T0354350

THE SPY

PAUL T WHITE

THE SPY

iUniverse books may be ordered through booksellers or by contacting:

iUniverse
1663 Liberty Drive
Bloomington, IN 47403
www.iuniverse.com
1-800-Authors (1-800-288-4677)

ISBN: 978-1-5320-2813-7 (sc)
ISBN: 978-1-5320-2815-1 (hc)
ISBN: 978-1-5320-2814-4 (e)

Print information available on the last page.

iUniverse rev. date: 07/08/2017

The Spy

a novel
by

PAUL T WHITE

I T WAS FIRST LIGHT, THE sun was not yet over the horizon but it was fading the stars and the reflected light was giving form to the desert.

He was not there and suddenly he was, running flat out. When he came to small obstacles he would leap over them and when he came to large obstacles like boulders or desert growth, he would veer to his left or right and then come right back on course, he was running a straight line across the desert. He ran but he did not seem to be straining or even breathing hard.

If there was more light you could see he had close cropped light brown hair and light brown eyes his body could be the model for sculpting the perfect humane form, he was butt naked.

He ran for 3.56 miles and stopped at the edge of a four lane divided highway. Across the highway there was a truck stop with a covered fuel island and a cluster of store fronts. He stood studying the buildings for a moment and then he started running to his right.

If there was anyone to see him, they could see his movement but there not enough light to see details. He came to the buildings and moved up under the overhang, walking fast to the rear of the building, he turned and moved down the building until he came to a door, He stopped, put his hand on the door knob and stood concentrating for a moment, he turned the knob and the door opened, as he stepped through the door, he turned and looking over his shoulder he saw a camera pointed directly at him, he continued through the door walking directly to the alarm system and turned it off. He turned, surveying the room, it was a dry goods store. The only thing he wore resembling clothing were a pair of socks covering the bottom of his feet, looking at them you could see they looked like nothing on this planet earth, they were strong as steel and pliable as cotton he knew exactly what he wanted, he walked to the clothing section and found the stacks of underwear, he rummage through the stacks until he found his size and ripped the plastic packaging off and dropped it on the floor, he put the underwear on and turned to the stacks of blue jeans, he disturbed the stacks until he found his size and put them on, he chose a light grey long sleeve dress shirt and buttoned it up as he walked to the shoes, he found his size in a walking shoe, he put them on over the socks he wore to protect the bottom of his feet, leaving the box and tissue paper on the floor, he stepped over to a full length mirror and stood studying his reflection for a moment then turned for the alarm system, he paused at a rack of belts, found his size, ripped the price tag off and dropped it on the floor, he laced the belt in the jeans as he walked to the alarm system.

At the alarm system he rewound the tape fifteen minutes and reset the alarm giving himself three minutes to get out of the door and he hurried out, retracing his steps to the front of the building. The sun was over the horizon, an automobile in the opposite lane was going west, it's headlights still on. He turned and walked slowly towards the fuel pumps, staying in the shadows closed to the building. There was a lighted convenience store across from the fuel pumps and he knew there would be a clerk in there but he had no money of any kind so he stopped and stood in the shadows and waited.

He looked up at the approach of a motor vehicle and watched an older pickup truck pull into the lot and stop at the fuel pump. The light blue paint on the truck was faded under a thin layer of dust and as he watched, the driver got out walked around the truck, put a credit card in the pump, put the hose in the truck, put the automatic on and stood back watching the meter tick over, her back was turned towards him. He stood studying the back of her head and then slowly he stepped off the curb and walked towards the pickup truck.

As Bonnie Steward stood watching the meter tick over, you would have a hard time guessing her 29 years, she still had her teenage figure with a flat stomach and high firm breast. She wore designer jeans and if they were not tailored for her, she spent a lot of time rummaging through the racks for this pair, they had been through the wash and they were just starting to fade, they fit her beautifully, leaving no doubt about the beautiful body she had.

She wore a matching button down the front long sleeve blouse that was open just enough to show her cleavage. She wore small silver ear rings that matched her belt buckle, her shoulder length sun bleached hair was tied back with a piece of rawhide string, a concession to her western heritage. She wore open sandals and stood just over five feet, her name matched her cornflower blue eyes, she wore just a touch of lipstick, everything about her was feminine.

He was close enough to her now and he said, "Good morning," flashing his most charming smile.., "Oh hello, I didn't see you," she said and the pump suddenly snapped off, she turned and gave the handle another squeeze, it snapped off again, she put the hose back in the pump, closed the cap on her tank and turned to him.

He smiled at her again, "my name is Neil Conrad, are you going into the city?"

"Bonnie," she returned his smile, normally she would never let a strange man get into her truck but as she stood staring into his eyes she suddenly knew she could trust this man without question. "Sure," she said, "hop in."

She turned walked around to the drivers side and got in, she opened the window and started the engine, She glanced over at him as he settled into the passenger seat, she pulled over to the highway looked over her shoulder and pulled out onto the highway, she close the window as she brought the truck up to speed and glanced over at him again.

"I like to use the air-conditioner, I don't like the sand and grit in my hair, I just washed it," she said.

Sounds like a good idea he said with a smile in his voice and he noticed the cab was the cleanest part of the truck.

She got the truck up to speed and settled down in the right hand lane, she glanced over at him "what do you do? she asked with a smile.

"I'm a pilot," he answered.

"Oh that's great, I've often wished I could do that, it must be great," she said.

"Yes it is" he said smiling over at her.

"My dad owns a small ranch back there," she nodded towards the rear of the truck as she said this.

"I had to make a forced landing in the desert back there," he said, continuing the conversation.

She took her eyes off the road and glanced over at him with a curious expression, but he was suddenly preoccupied studying the side rear view mirror, "there is a siren back there," he said, turning to glance at her.

She turned to look at the highway and glance at the rear view mirror, "I don't see anything," she said.

"There is a pick-up truck coming very fast, he will pass you on the left," he said staring into the side mirror.

"I see him," she said glancing into the rear view mirror, she took her foot off the gas and steered the truck to the extreme right side of her lane, the pick-up passed them on the left with a 'whoosh' and continued on, the driver had the truck wide open. Neil took his eyes off the side mirror and watched the pick-up fast disappearing in front of them.

A large billboard sign was on the right of the highway up ahead and as he watched the speeding pick-up come even with the sign he saw a black object fly out of the pick-up and land among the desert growth at the bottom of the sign, he glanced back at the mirror and saw flashing lights and the siren was unmistakable now, here he comes, passing on your left," he said.

"Whoosh" the patrol car passed them on their left, the siren screaming.

"Wooo," she said exhaling, she steered back to the middle of her lane.

"Pull over an stop at that sign," he said.

She looked over at him and saw the determination on his face and began to slow the truck, she pulled off the road and stopped at the sign, he opened his door, stepped over the shallow ditch and bent over searching among the growth under the sign, he turned and started back to the truck with a black bag in his hand. He got into the truck and with

4

the bag between his feet he pulled the zipper back exposing neat bundles of U.S. currency, he glanced over at her, she was grinning wide eyed at the bag. He turned back to the bag and began to pull out the currency digging to the bottom, The bottom was covered with a plastic bag, he pulled it out, it was filled with white powder, he held the bag in both hands and pulled on each side, it was heavy duty polyethylene, it did not tear, it stretched, he looked over at her and ask if she had a knife or scissors, she shook her head no, watching him with interest. He turned and opened the glove compartment and pulled out a rusty screwdriver, he held the bag between his knees and pulling on it with his left hand, he dug the screwdriver into the plastic, the plastic tore, the screwdriver slipped and cut a gash in his left hand between the thumb and forefinger, he stopped and stared at the cut as the blood formed, suddenly it stopped and slowly began to disappear, he continued to stare at the cut, the flesh came together.

He turned his attention back to the bag, he stuck his index finger in the hole and held it to his nose, "narcotics," he said and then held his finger for her to smell, "cocaine," she said looking over at him confirming his find.

Carrying the bag he opened the door, stepped into the ditch and began to shake the cocaine on the ground, kicking sand and dirt over as he went, when the bag was empty he put it on the ground and covered one end with dirt, he turned, got back into the truck and rearranged the black bag between his feet and turned to her, she had been watching him with intense interest.

"We had better get out o here," he said.

She came to life reached down and fired the engine and steered back on the highway and pressed the gas bringing the truck up to the speed limit, she divided her attention between the highway and glancing over at him as he pulled each bundle of cash out of the bag, thumbed each stack and made two piles on the dashboard.

When the bag was empty he looked over at her and ask, "do you have a purse?"

She reached behind her seat and handed him a large bag with a shoulder strap, he began to fill the bag with half of the currency and handed it back to her, she put the purse behind her seat then glanced back at him as he put the other half of the currency back in the bag and closed the zipper. She looked at his left hand again, there was just a red scar where the cut had been.

"You are not from around here are you?" she ask.

He waited for a moment before he answered and then said, "no, no I am not, I came from a planet on the other side of the galaxy."

She turned looked into his eyes for a instant and then looked back at the highway.

"There is about twenty five thousand dollars here, you have about twelve thousand five hundred in your purse and the rest is in this bag." he waited for this to sink in and then he continued, "Bonnie I Need your help, will you help me?"

Bonnie turned looked into his eyes then glanced at his left hand, the red scar was disappearing, she turned her eyes back to the highway and after a moment of silence she said, "yes, yes i Will," she turned and met his eyes again.

He settled back in his seat and began to explain, "when we first ventured into space from our planet we saw that our microelectronics were being threatened by solar flares and radiation belts in space so our scientist were put to work on the problem. They came up with an electronic shield, when the shield was on, the rays came at the ship and just bent around it and kept on going. At first the shield took a lot of energy and the shields were turned off when the ships were brought back to to the planet but they improved on the method until a ship landed with the shield up and it was very difficult to see the ship and they discovered the shield bent light rays as well as solar flares radiation and radar, They continued to work with the problem until we became invisible.., Bonnie I Know how complicated this is to understand..."

"No, no we have stealth fighters and bombers now that are almost invisible to radar, we have had them for a number of years and the science has probably advanced a lot farther then the public knows," Bonnie said.

"Yes you have," he said glancing over with a smile and then he continued, "my ship is brand new, it's almost a prototype, I was having trouble with the engine and I called the mother ship, they are over at another solar system with a problem of their own and they can not get here for five sunsets so I decided to land in the desert so no one would see the ship, the problem is I'm using the generator for the shield and the main engine fuel can not be used for the generator, I have about three more days of fuel for the generator.

"What happens when you run out of fuel?" She ask.

"The generator will slowly stop, the shield will come down and you will be able to look out there and see a space ship sitting in the desert," he explained.

"But I don't understand, why don't you just go to NASA and tell them who you are, I'm sure they would welcome you with open arms," she said. "No we cain't do that, you are not ready yet.., I could probably give them some tips on building a better space ship, tips on space travel in general but when it comes to things like how to grow drought resistant crops or how to prevent destructive storms, I wouldn't be much help and all these things must come together at the same time," he explained.

Bonnie sat dividing her attention between looking at the road, glancing over at him and glancing in the rear view mirror, he had her attention.

"Let me give an example," he continued, "when motor vehicles replaced the horse drawn carriage and all the waste from the animals was removed, it improved humane health, this was especially true in the cities so you see the internal combustion engine advanced medicine.

With the morning progressing they were beginning to see more traffic, she took her eyes off the road and quickly glanced at him, "Yes, I see," she said.

"Of the five days I have until I can get some help, I have already used two days getting used to your oxygen and gravity, I figure I have three more days before the generator stops." he explained. "I need about 100 pounds of bituminous coal," he added.

"Coal! that's primitive isn't it?" she said.

"I have some chemicals on board that will convert it to a liquid, it will burn clean, the only exhaust will be excess heat," he said, after a moment he continued, the reason I came here, this place is an area with a number of large coal burning power plants, a lot of rail lines with rail cars carrying coal come here." He said.

Yes that would be the four corners area, but that's a good ways from here, maybe we can find a coal burning power plant closer," She said.

Conversation in the truck was difficult with the noise, even with the windows closed and the traffic was becoming heavier and she concentrated on the road while he sat back and observed the life around him.

They suddenly came over a rise in the desert floor and there in the distance on their left a town was spread out, they both sat studying the vista without speaking, she glanced at her watch, "are you hungry?" "Do you want to stop and eat?" she ask.

He had been concentrating on the horizon, looking for a tall smokestack or chimney, he turned to her and said, "Yes" and then he saw the chimney over on the far side of the town, he doubted if she could see it yet so he waited.

There was an off ramp leading off the highway that would carry them into the town, she took her foot off the gas and began to slow, after they made their turn he began to study the horizon and there it was, closer now, he turned to her, "there is a large smokestack," he said.

"Where?" She ask turning her head. He pointed it out for her.

She sat with her eyes on the highway glancing at the chimney. "It's a good ways over there, the desert dips down and you can see the tops of cooling towers farther on, they could be burning oil or natural gas but from the size of it, they are probably burning coal," she said.

"Yes I agree," he comments.

"We may as well eat first and plan how we will handle this," she glanced at the gas gauge, "and we may as well top off the gas tank while we are here," she said keeping her eyes on the road, looking for a gas station.

She spotted one up ahead and pulled in, she jumped out with her credit card and quickly had the fuel hose in the truck with the automatic on. With the tank full she got back in the cab and he pointed at a fast food restaurant up ahead.

"No," she said, "let's find something better," they could not see the tower from where they were but she drove on bearing to her right in the direction she last saw the tower, she saw a small red neon sign ahead,

8

"Ben's Steaks," it was over the door of a one story bungalow set in the middle of a parking lot.

"This looks good and the parking lot is almost full, that is usually a good sign," she said as she turned into the lot looking for a place to park.

They stood waiting to be seated, she had the strap of her purse on her left shoulder and he carried the bag in his left hand, they were escorted to a table, the light was low even for midday, the tables had white tablecloths and the dinning room was almost full but the diners all spoke in low tones while the waitresses and waiters moved about silently among the tables. Bonnie excused herself for the ladies room and the waitress left menus. He sat and without staring studied the other diners, the way they used their silverware and where they put the napkins. Bonnie was back and he put the menu down as Bonnie sat and whispered, "if you need the men's room it's over there," she nodded towards a corner of the room.

He looked at her, "I can read this," he indicated the menu, "but I don't understand what it means, why don't you order for me while I go to the men's room?" He reached down and moved the bag closer to her and made sure she knew it was there. "Are you hungry?" She ask as he stood, he glanced down and said, "yes," then turned for the men's room.

He returned to the table, the waitress had water and ice tea on the table. "I ordered you a steak," said Bonnie as he sat down, he looked at her and nodded then reached for the ice water and drained the glass, "that's good water," he said, Bonnie smiled at him and said, "ice tea," as she reached for her glass and removed the lemon slice and squeezed it into the glass, he studied her every move and watched her reach for the sugar bowl, the pink ones are artificial sugar for people who want to restrict their sugar, the white ones are sugar," she explained.

He sat trying to be as subtle as possible while he watched her every move.

Bonnie does not stop and try to understand what is going on with this handsome man, she just goes along with him, she believes what he says,

it explains everything and there is no reason not to believe him and he is a quick learner.

The waitress is back with a basket of warm dinner rolls wrapped in a napkin, Bonnie takes one, breaks off a piece puts spread on it and puts it in her mouth. She chews and watches him copy her moves, "dinner rolls.., yeast rolls," she says.

He nods chewing, the waitress brings salads, a large one for Bonnie a smaller one for him, he picked up the fork, left hand, knife in the right and he begins, the steak arrives still sizzling with french fries, Bonnie watches him clean the plate then sit back and use his napkin, "do you want desert?" She ask, he nods with indifference, She orders a chocolate fudge sundae, halfway through he stops and uses his napkin. Bonnie had finished her salad and she sat watching him and she could see he had his fill and she leaned forward and whispered, "I'll get the bill."

The waitress came with a small tray with the bill on it, he had opened one of the stacks of bills from the bag and put a roll of bills in his left front pocket, the waitress put the tray down and left, he pulled out the roll and peeled off three twenties and put them on the tray, Bonnie watched and took one of the twenties back and handed it to him and whispered, "that's plenty and there will be a nice tip." He took the twenty back and nodded at her as he replaced the bill on the roll. Then he whispered, "I think I will go to the men's room again."

When Bonnie saw him coming back she put her purse on her shoulder and picked up the bag and handed it to him when he got to the table, they turned and walked out. He had been studying english and life on planet earth for some time and now he could say he has joined the inhabitants and eaten their food. As they stepped out of the front door he leaned over and whispered, "I can understand why there is such a problem with overweight and obesity here," she looked at him and nodded with a grin.

Bonnie pulled out of the parking lot and continued to bear right at each intersection. They came to an open field it was a recreation area, "there it is," said Bonnie.

"Yes and there are the cooling towers in the back, they must be burning coal, that's a conveyer belt, they unload the coal back there and bring it up here to the furnace," he explained.

The complex was surrounded by a high chain link fence, a guard shack was at the entrance gate, Bonnie pulled up to the shack, a guard came out with a clip board in his hand, he looked into the empty truck bed then turned his attention to the cab, bending over, looking in, he took note of the bag between Neil's feet.

"Good Day," he said.

"Hello," said Bonnie, "we are here to see the manager."

"I'll check," Said the guard, "What's your business?"

"We need to talk to him about his coal supply," said Neil from the passenger seat.

"What's your name," said the guard, poised with the pen ready to write.

Bonnie gave her name, the guard wrote it down and said, "just a minute,"

he turned, walked into the shack picked up the phone spoke briefly and came back out to the truck, he still had the clip board in his left hand and he pointed the clip board at a building and said, "park over there and follow the signs to his office.

"Thanks," said Bonnie giving him her most winning smile.

She parked the truck and they got out and walked into the door with the small black and white sign that read manager. The receptionist looked up, she had been expecting them since the phone call from the guard.

"Good morning, we are here to see the manager," said Bonnie as she led the way.

The receptionist stood and smiling stepped over to a door and opened it, she looked in then stood back holding the door open for them, Bonnie continued to lead the way.

It was a typical managers office, the walls on each side were lined with file cabinets the wall behind the desk had glass windows looking onto the slowly moving conveyer belt that carried the coal to the furnace. The manager sat at his desk in shirt sleeves, he looked up as they entered.

"Hello," said Bonnie, "we are here to see about buying some coal."

The manager sat looking at them in silence for a moment then said, "we buy coal, we don't sell it."

Neil had the folded bills out of his pocket as he walked over to the edge of the desk, "we are experimenting with a generator and we need about one hundred pounds of coal," as he said this he peeled off one hundred dollar bills and fanned them out on the edge of the desk, when he got to five he stopped and looked into the manager's eyes.

The manager quickly looked around then looked down at the bills on the edge of his desk, he stood and looked into Neil's eyes and said, "tomorrow is Saturday, most of the people will not be here but I have to come in, come back in the morning," then with a wave of his hand he indicated Neil should take the money with him. Neil picked up the bills and turned for the door.

"Come back about nine O'clock," said the manager to Neil's back.

Neil half turned and said, "O.K., nine o'clock, we will be here," Then he held the door for Bonnie.

Neil waved at the guard as Bonnie drove slowly through the gate, "I'll drive down to the center of town and park so we can talk," Bonnie said keeping her eyes on the road.

The center of town had a park two blocks by one block, the park ran north south and there were walkways with grass and large shade trees, shade trees were also in front of store fronts that lined the park on both sides and there was parallel parking. Bonnie pulled up and parked under a shade tree and opened her window.

"I was watching his eyes and I think he wants to sell the coal," said Bonnie.

"Yes I think you are right," he said as he rolled down his window," This means we will have to spend the night and wait until morning.

"I think it will be better if we stay together.., check into a hotel or motel," She said.

"How will that work?" He ask.

"Just take your bag," she indicated the bag between his feet, "it will pass as an overnight bag and just go in and sign Mr. & Mrs, you can use any name you want and pay cash, that way they cain't trace anything.

· They sat thinking this over for a moment and then Bonnie ask, "do you want to walk over there and sit on that bench in the shade?"

It was late summer and the afternoon heat was building but the air was dry and in the shade they could sit and talk, there was a slight breeze, enough to move the air and the leaves on the large poplar tree they sat under.

They sat on the bench facing south, he had placed the bag on the bench between them, she noticed he seemed a bit pensive, his thoughts somewhere else what's the matter?" she ask.

He turned to her and smiled, "oh I saw something back there that reminded me of an incident that happened a long time ago," he explained.

"Was it bad?" she ask.

"No .., uh, back when I first joined the exploration Corps, I was a cadet, just a kid, just starting to shave, we were at a place that was used for maneuvers, the land has never been used for cultivation, It is covered with purple sage and it is a long way from the nearest town, they had a rail line that ran by the place but it was seldom used and there was a short platform with a small shack for the station. I had some leave coming and I was there to check on times and schedules, I looked up and saw an officer approaching, he had a woman by his side, I was standing there trying to remember all the protocol for addressing a senior officer and then I saw he was a field grade officer and my mind really got busy trying to remember all the protocol for the occasion, when they were close enough I snapped to attention and gave one of my best hand salutes, he returned this fluttering indifferent thing and ask, "is this the train station?"

"Yes sir it is," I answered, still rigidly at attention.

"That was all it took to identify me as coming from the region I came from,

there had been some wars there and a lot of hatred pass down from parent to offspring and even after a lot of time had passed, there were still strong feelings. The woman burst out in laughter at my answer and the Officer chuckled along with her."

"The Officer was not in the Exploration Corps, I think he was in the Quartermaster Corps," he continued to explain, "we in the Exploration Corps were a rigid and very highly disciplined unit and there are other units that have the same uniform the same ranks the same gold on their epaulets but they are just lax when it comes to discipline, we in the Exploration Corps were accustomed to company grade officers, we treated them like demigods but a field grade officer, that was not God himself but one of his first assistant and the idea of a field grade officer humiliating the lower ranks like that just was not done.

"It seems to me I have heard that story before or one very much like it,"

said Bonnie.

"Yes it's remarkable," he said.

"Remarkable?" Bonnie repeated glancing over at him.

"Yes remarkable or the equivalent word in my language is used a lot in describe new planets we explore, new planets where life has progressed to the point of civilization. On planet earth here, it's like going to a different nation, the language and customs are different but the people are the same, it's just humanity with all the same problems, It's remarkable."

"I hear that and I am back to why you cain't just go to NASA or the government and say who you are and give them the benefit of your knowledge?" Bonnie asked.

"To be brutally frank Bonnie, you are just not ready yet..," he paused before continuing.

"Bonnie you have the beginning of what you need, you have the United Nations, now you need a strong and completely selfless leader in the U.N., he needs to be less concerned about wealth and personal power and more concerned about his legacy as the man who went into the United Nations and finally made it what it was meant to be."

"Your nations have got to stop wasting their treasuries on sectarian wars and contribute to the U.N. Army, give them a uniform they can be proud of, pay them a good wage, demand loyalty and station them around the planet and if one nation infringes on another, send in an overpowering force and put a stop to it. Planet earth will need all it's treasure to venture into space," he added.

"There is a vocal minority here who say we should not be going into space, we should take care of the problems here on earth first," said Bonnie.

This was met with a moment of silence as he collected his thoughts..,
"Bonnie there are many, many, planets out there with water, planets where the bombardment from comets and asteroids has ceased and

photosynthesis has started and life has just begun. All of these planets can be colonized, and in fact they will be by someone, can you visualize going to a virgin planet and colonizing it with the knowledge you have here on earth, do it without all the pollution, you could build a paradise, the treasure out there is beyond the imagination of most of the citizens on earth."

"THere is another reason you must go, perhaps the biggest reason of all..,

life changes, everything changes, granite is worn away by wind and weather, everything changes and planet earth is changing, you moon is moving away from earth, it's moving very slowly but it is moving away and this will change life here on earth.., everything changes and you must get organized and make one effort by planet earth to venture out past your solar system.

He paused again and said, "there is treasure and adventure out there for everyone, but you have to go, you have to get organized and go."

The only time Bonnie thought about space was when NASA did something that made headlines, otherwise she spent her time and energy on herself, on life, but as she sat listening to this man she could understand the logic of what he was saying.

"Bonnie my planet is only eight hundred to one thousand years ahead of planet earth and that gap is closing very fast now and when you are ready to venture into space, go outside your solar system, it will take the efforts and contributions of all of your nations working together and when you are ready you will be contacted," he explained.

Bonnie sat taking this all in, thinking about what he was saying, it wasn't profoundly new but it was the first time she had heard it spoken of in this way.

"The first law of the Exploration Corps, the first rule is to never leave anything behind, never leave anything that can be pointed at and said there see that, that is proof they were here." he explained.

He stopped speaking for a moment and his hand came up and rested on the bag between them.., "Bonnie another thing that is taught from a very early age on my planet is sex education."

He paused again collecting his thoughts and then he continued, "they knew from the beginning that sex was an important part of life, almost a necessary part and they also knew it could be suppressed, so they lectured from the pulpit and with advertising about the evils of sex such as out of wedlock childbirth and sexually transmitted disease and so on, hoping to control the population and leave the sex education to the family. Then they learned even with the lectures the youth were having sex anyway so they stopped the lectures and began to educate the youth from the earliest age and as they grew and matured the sex education matured with them and by the time they reached puberty, there were no surprises and when they finished primary school, your high school, they know all there is to know about sex."

"Did that put an end to the problems with sex," Bonnie ask.

"No" he quickly answered, "because sex is such a deeply personal thing and because some find it easier to suppress then others, out of wedlock pregnancies still turn up but now they can go to the government and get the best possible care but they have to give up the child and if there is a second out of wedlock pregnancy they cain't claim they didn't know better and they have to give up the baby and undergo surgery to prevent any further pregnancies."

He paused then added, "what it did do was prevent 12 year olds from teaching the facts of life to 8 and 9 year olds."

"Getting married is one of the most difficult things to do on my planet," he continued, if you want to get married and start a family you have to apply for a license and show you can financially afford to take care of a family as well as provide for them into the future and then you have to go into counseling with your partner this can take nine months or longer, it can take until you and your partner are sure you know each other and there are no more marriages because of out of wedlock pregnancies because this leads to all kinds of problems."

"There must be a lot of living together without benefit of marriage," said Bonnie.

"Yes," he answered, "but it cuts down on population growth because without legal citizenship you can not take advantage of all the benefits the government has to offer and without that life would be unthinkable.., sex has many benefits, it relieves stress, it lets you sleep, and live longer, It boost your immune system, in short it makes life interesting and worth living."

The sun was slipping farther to the west and the heat was giving way to the cooler air in the shadows, Neil paused from speaking for a moment and then he continued.

"Another thing they do during primary education is take the D.N.A. of each student and study their genes and determine where their talents and gifts lie, to give an example if a student has a gift for public speaking they would steer him or her into law or politics but at the same time if that student wanted to be an entrepreneur, they would not interfere with that. In my case, my genes allow me to live for long periods without the company of others and with my other talents and gifts I was steered into the Exploration Corps."

There was silence and he sat in contemplation for a moment and then he began to speak, "Bonnie there is one more reason I can not stay on this planet," he paused then turned to her, "I calculate I am one hundred and twenty three earth years old."

Bonnie sat silent for a moment looking at him and then said, "and I have been sitting here wondering if I am too old for you!"

"Bonnie you are just a child," he said smiling at her.

"Hah, don't I wish," said Bonnie, throwing her head back with laughter.

After a pause he began to explain, "many years ago people on my planet began to die by the thousands, it was from pulmonary and other diseases, there were a lot of arguments pro and con as to the cause, some said it was the pollution others said it was a natural occurrence that it had happened before and of course the strongest arguments came from the people who were profiting from the pollution and nothing was done until the figures of the dead and dying reached into the hundreds of thousands and the people with the strongest arguments that it was a natural occurrence realized the planet was dying and something had to be done. The government put an immediate ban on the burning of fossil fuel, the ban included everything except power generation and there were sever penalties for anyone caught not observing the ban, at first there was serious unemployment but the continued high death rates eased that and the dying continued so they built large chimneys," he nodded in the direction of the power plant they just visited, "and they began to pump oxygen into the lower atmosphere and the wind and

17

rain slowly began to clean the atmosphere but the death rates continued, so they began to experiment with gases that had special antibiotic properties and they mixed that with the oxygen and pumped it into the atmosphere and slowly the dying began to stabilize, they continued pumping and the terrible figures of the dying began to come down and the rain and wind slowly cleaned the atmosphere,"

He paused for a moment and then continued, "they noticed the population was healthier and after some time they saw the the life span was increasing, "Neil continued to explain, "the atmosphere on my planet has completely changed from oxygen and the other gases from fossil fuel and so on to oxygen and antibiotics of today.., the population is healthier and the life span on my planet is estimated to be two hundred years."

He paused thinking for a moment and then continued, "Bonnie you are aware the farther away from planet earth's gravity you get the slower you age?"

There was silence and then Bonnie answered, "I think I've heard that, I think it is in Albert Einstein's theory of relativity but I don't think anyone has proven it yet."

"Well it's true," he said, "they have artificial or created gravity on the mothership and they are working to prove whether that gravity will stop aging or not, my Exploration Corps ship is too small so being away from a planets gravity keeps me young and prime, I have to exercise and keep moving, I have a special exercise machine on the ship, and special medications I have to take about once a week, to help bone growth and so forth."

He looked over at her and said, "Bonnie if I stayed here on earth in a matter of months I would start to look my true age in earth years and in a couple of years if I lasted that long I would just be a dried up old man who looked every bit as old as I would be in Earth years."

After a moment of silence his head came up and he looked around, "Bonnie it's getting late, how is this, this hotel room going to work again?"

Bonnie looked up, "Well we will just go and sign the register as Mr. & Mrs."

"Is that all there is to it?" "I mean will they ask for identification," he said, then he added, "I don't have a thing on me."

Bonnie thought for a moment, "well in other countries they require that you leave your passports with the front desk, but we don't have passports here.., it's possible they could ask for identification.., alright, I'll sign the register, you pay cash, if they ask for I.D. I'll show them my drivers license, they can trace my name but so what, if they want to arrest us, they'll have to arrest three quarters of the population."

"O.K., sounds good but remember the first rule of the Exploration Corps," he said.

She looked at him and nodded then said, "let's walk to the other end of the park."

At the south end of the park there was a hotel from another era, it was a rectangular red brick building with white windows, you would not count the floors but it was eight stories high and there was a lighted sign on the roof that read "Mayflower Hotel." They walked together to the end of the park, crossed the street and walked to the hotel, there were two large plate glass windows with an old fashioned double door in the middle, through the plate glass could be seen the lobby with stuffed leather furniture and potted plants, Bonnie saw a menu taped to the corner of the plate glass on the left and she stepped over and began to read, she joined him again and they walked on.

"They have a dinning room and the menu looks good, we can check in and just stay off the street until morning, the lobby looks comfortable," she added.

He switched the bag to his left hand and they walked closer together, "O.K. sounds good," he said.

"Let's walk back down to the truck and bring it up here," she said, they came to a drug store and Bonnie stopped and said "lets go in here. "

They came out of the drug store with their purchases and continued down to the truck.

Bonnie carried a small shopping bag in her hand, she purchased toilet articles, tooth brushes, lotion, soap, etc; and she purchased disposable razors and a shaving soap for him, They drove the truck down and parked it parallel to the curb opposite the hotel.

They walked to the front desk, he carrying the black bag, and she had the shopping bag, Bonnie ask the clerk if they had a vacancy and the response was "yes," as he placed a register card in front of her and she began to fill out the form as the clerk hovered, Neil put the bag on the floor and ask the clerk how much as he pulled the folded bills out of his pocket, the clerk looked up and gave him a figure, "that's one night," said the clerk. Bonnie finished filling out the card and slid it over as Neil began counting the bills out. The clerk briefly read the card, looked up beaming and picked up the money Neil had placed on the counter, he turned and handed them an old fashion hotel key and said, that will be on the fifth floor, do you have bags?" "No said Bonnie, we can find it," as she picked up the key and turned for the elevator. The clerk beamed another smile as he watched them walk away.

"Well that was easy enough," said Neil as he used the key to open the door.

"Yes," said Bonnie, "I used my real name and just put down a rural post office box number for a home address."

The room was a bit old fashion like the rest of the hotel but it was large, clean and comfortable, with twin beds, Bonnie walked into the bathroom with the bag from the drugstore. She came out and Neil stood at the window, his fingers propping open the slats on the blinds, he looked down and said, "we are overlooking the park, I can see the truck."

Bonnie moved close to him and peered out, he said, "mmm, you really smell good, she held her finger up then stepped over and picked up the phone, she recognized the clerks voice, he was doing double duty, "Hello this is Mrs. Steward I just checked in and I forgot to ask, we parked out front is that O.K.?"

"Yes," answered the clerk, "we have a lot out back but I am sure you will be alright there."

"Thank you," Bonnie hung up the phone, then turned to Neil and said, well I think we will be alright as long as we stay here in the hotel until morning.., and it's my favorite scent you smell, they had a sale on it at the drug store and I bought you a razor and some soap so we don't have to go out until we are ready to go to the power company.

"That's good, I don't feel much like going out any way." Said Neil.

"Let me freshen up a little," said Bonnie as she turned for the bath.

Neil was sitting in the chair next to the window he had turned the lights on, she came out, "do you want to freshen up?" "Yes," he answered as he walked into the bathroom and closed the door.

He carried the bag with him as they rode the elevator down and walked across the lobby to the dinning room. The menu featured grilled salmon with a dill sauce, spiced rice and cooked vegetables, he was accustomed to the tableware now and the atmosphere was making him hungry.

Bonnie lay the menu on the edge of the table and said, "how about fish.., salmon?" Neil looked at her with an indifferent expression, they were two of the earliest diners, several tables were busy but the dinning room was mostly empty with waiters busy getting things ready for the dinner crowd.

A bus boy was filling the water glasses and then the waitress came and Bonnie ordered the salmon.

They sat back and waited while the waitress was busy with dinner rolls, ice tea, etc; "You said these new planets were photosynthesis and life is just beginning and they will have to be colonized, why is that, why are they not just left alone, left to progress on their on?" Bonnie ask just above a whisper.

He sat thinking about her question, "in the past they helped other planets," he began to explain, "planets who had progressed close to the point where earth is now, they gave them technology and the planet got to squabbling over who would be in charge and sectarian wars broke out and they had just enough technology to start killing each other and the planet reverted back to pure savagery and finally they decided to leave them aloneand hope the planet would get back to some kind of civilization.

He took a large swallow of water and then continued just above a whisper, "just outside this galaxy there is a very sinister and evil force, we have not met them yet, but we have been just where they left and apparently they kill and destroy for the sport or amusement of it, we know they have as much technology as we do, maybe more but that is all we know about them, we don't know what they eat, we don't know what they want, the advanced planets in this galaxy have formed a federation for self protection and planet earth will be contacted.

They finished dinner and took the elevator back to the room, he carried the bag like a diplomatic pouch absent the chain and cuffs attached to his wrist.

Entering the room he announced he would take a shower, after about fifteen minutes the door opened and he came out wearing a towel about his waist, it came down to the tops of his thighs and he carried his jeans and shirt folded on his arm. Bonnie stood at the window with her cell phone, she looked at him and clicked the phone off.

"I just called my Dad and told him I would be staying in town tonight," she said. Looking at him dressed in the towel, she saw what a magnificent specimen he really was. She stepped over to her purse and put the phone in and took out a condom and place it on the pillow of the closest twin bed, she looked at him with a mischievous grin and said, "in case you change your mind," she turned and walked into the bathroom and closed the door.

Shortly, she came out, she wore a towel wrapped around her breast and it came down to the top of her thighs. He had folded the dust cover down on one of the beds and he lay there under a sheet, he looked at her smiling and without speaking, threw the sheet back, inviting her into the bed, she, grinning slipped the towel off and draped it across the back of a chair then moved towards the bed and lay down besides him, he took her in his arms and slowly kissed her.

She pulled back grinning, "you are the first one hundred and twenty three year old man I ever kissed."

"Yes and if my superiors find out about this, they will lock me up for robbing the cradle," he chuckled and then kissed her again.

She giggled in his ear and returned the kiss.

The next morning the bathroom door was closed, he had made all his moves, used all his techniques and Bonnie sat in the bed watching the morning news on television, her cute little right nipple just peeping over the sheet gathered under her breast Bonnie was a happy and completely satisfied woman.

The bathroom door opened and Neil came out dressed in his jeans and dress shirt. Bonnie looked at him and threw the sheet back saying, "there isn't much news on the television this morning," as she walked to the bathroom and closed the door.

After ten minutes Bonnie came out of the bathroom dressed, Neil stood at the window, two fingers propping the the blind opened as he peered out, he looked at her and said, "looks like we may have a problem," Bonnie stepped over and peered out, as they watched, a police officer got out of a police car that had pulled up behind the pickup. He walked slowly, looking into the truck bed then stopped and looked into the cab, Neil pulled his fingers out of the blind and said, "O.K. we will act normal, act like nothing has happened, we'll go down to breakfast and if anyone ask any questions just act normal."

"Right," said Bonnie, "but he is probably just routine checking, there is a lot of narcotic smuggling that goes on this close to the border and he is probably just routinely checking."

"O.K. well just act normal," said Neil.

They took the elevator to the lobby and walked to the dinning room, Neil glanced at the front desk, the clerk was bent over with some routine work and he did not look up. They were quickly seated sipping coffee and juice as they waited for their order.

"I was married once,' said Bonnie, "we were just kids and luckily we broke it off before we had children, I left school for a while then went back and finished, I have a degree in liberal arts with a major in drama."

The waitress came with their order and Neil got busy with the food in front of him pausing to ask, "have you worked as an actress?"

"No, when we met, I was going into town to do some shopping for a trip to Los Angeles, I have the name of an agent and I was hoping he could find some work for me," Bonnie explained.

Neil took a couple of bites from the eggs and sausage then finished a stack of pancakes. Bonnie looked at him and ask, "are the eggs alright?"

"Yes, I'm just not in the mood, the diet on my planet is based on grains," he said.

"Oh, I should have ordered cooked cereal, would you like a bowl?"

"No I'm fine, I just wasn't as hungry as I thought," He explained.

The waitress approached carrying a coffee pot, Bonnie declined for both of them, the the waitress looked down at the eggs and sausage and ask, "were the eggs O.K.?"

"Yes the eggs were fine he just wasn't as hungry as he thought."

"Do you want the check?" ask the waitress.

"Yes answered Bonnie.

The waitress left and returned with the check, placing it on the table.

"Thank you," said Bonnie Neil looked at the bill and counted out some bills, leaving a nice tip, they started across the lobby, Neil glanced at the front desk, the clerk was watching them and he held up his hand when Neil looked at him, "wait just a minute," he said to Bonnie, touching her arm, Bonnie half turned and watched him walk towards the front desk.

"A police officer was checking on your truck," said the clerk when Neil was close enough, "I told him you were registered in the hotel and he seemed satisfied and he left."

"Good, thank you," said Neil as he half turned, then he turned back and said, "the breakfast was fine, the food was good."

The clerk beamed a smile, "thank You," he said.

"I was hoping it would be something like that," said Bonnie as the elevator door closed.

"Yes it's good to see they are doing their jobs," Neil replied.

Neil went into the bathroom right away, closing the door, he came out shortly, his shirt was off and his pants were fastened but his belt was unbuckled, he looked at Bonnie grinning, "do you have another prophylactic?" he ask.

"Yes I do," said Bonnie returning his grin, she stepped over to her purse, took out a prophylactic, placed it on the pillow and said, "give me a minute she turned for the bathroom and closed the door.

Later they lay in each others arms, "that was paradise right there," said Neil, whispering in her ear.., he kissed her again and said, "well I guess we had better go and see about buying some coal."

"Yes," said Bonnie throwing off the sheet, she walked into the bathroom and closed the door.

They checked out of the hotel and Bonnie retraced the route back o the power plant, Stopping at the front gate, the guard came out again carrying his clip board, he looked in the cab and saw the black bag between Neil's feet and he pointed to the same place as yesterday and Bonnie gave him her winning smile and pulled over and parked.

The receptionist's was off for the weekend and no one was in the room, Bonnie stepped over to the door to the inner office and tapped, "come in," answered a voice from inside, they filed into the room, the manager sat at his desk in his shirt sleeves, he looked up, "good morning, you are right on time," glancing at his watch, he then leaned back in his chair and said, "you said about one hundred pounds?"

"Yes said Neil as he stepped over to the desk and began to count out one hundred dollar bills and lay them on the desk.

Bonnie looking through the window saw the conveyer belt was full of coal but it was stopped.

"Do you have anything to carry it in?" The manager ask as he scooped up the bills an put them in the middle drawer "No," said Neil.

"Come with me," said the manager as he walked around his desk and led them through a side door onto a long ramp that paralleled the conveyer belt, he stopped at a locker and pulled out an old army duffle bag. He turned back towards his office and began to put large select pieces of coal into the bag, "You are right this is probably the only place to get coal anymore, you say you are experimenting with a new generator?"

"Yes," said Neil.

The duffle bag was becoming full and hard to carry, finally the manager stopped and turned to Neil, Neil reached over and picked one more large piece of coal about the size of his two fist and put it on top of the bag, pushed it down and closed the duffel, he reached into his pocket and pulled out the roll of bills and peeled off another one hundred dollar bill and handed it to the manager, "for the bag," he said. "It's not worth that said the manager," "It is to me said Neil.

The manager turned and led them back into the office, dusting his hands together he said, "it's been a pleasure doing business with you."

"Yes it's been a pleasure," said Neil as he lifted the bag with the middle handle and turned to go then turned back and said, "thank you," then turned for the door, Bonnie was behind him carrying the black bag.

Neil put the duffle bag in the truck bed up next to the cab and got back in the passenger side with the black bag between his feet.

Bonnie drove through the gate as Neil waved and smiled at the guard.

"That went well," said Bonnie.

"Yes," said Neil, "he seems like a pretty nice guy, maybe he can find a way to pay the company back."

They found the four lane highway leading out of town to the interstate Bonnie was in the outside slow lane, watching her speed, she glanced over at him with start of a smile on her lips, "so you like to live alone," She said.

He looked over at her and said, "Bonnie just because I can do that doesn't mean I like to do it or would choose to do it and that is never more true then when I am close to someone as beautiful as you."

Bonnie smiled at him then glanced back at the highway and began to slow for the entrance ramp leading up onto the interstate heading west.

Bonnie was glancing over her shoulder and looking into the rear view mirror as she picked up speed to match the interstate traffic, there were service stations and convenience stores clustered on the four corners of the interstate and they were just clearing the last one before the highway entered the open desert.

"That was a police car back there," said Neil.

"It's O. K., I'm in the speed limit," said Bonnie as she glanced at the speedometer and then at the rear view mirror and back at the highway..,

"Uh oh, and here he comes," she said looking in the rearview mirror.

Neil sat watching the police car in his side view mirror.

The police car came right up behind them and the driver turned on all his lights.

"Hand me the registration in the white envelop," Bonnie indicated the glove compartment, "Let me try to handle this," she added as she slowed and found a spot to pull clear of the highway, She reached behind her seat for her purse then dug out her wallet and found her driver's license as she watched a tall thin black police officer get out of the police car and walk slowly towards them, he wore dark aviator style sunglasses.

Bonnie opened her window as the police officer walked up, "what's the problem?" ask Bonnie.

"Let me see your driver's license and registration," said the police officer.

Bonnie handed them through the window. The police officer stood slowly reading the documents, Neil sat quietly waiting. Finally the officer looked in the window and said, "do you want to step out of the truck?" "What's this all about," said Bonnie as she opened her door and stepped out.

"I stopped you as a suspicious vehicle," said the officer, "what's in the duffel," he ask as he turned and walked back around the truck bed, he still carried Bonnie's drivers license and registration in his left hand.

"Hah, I'd like to stand before a judge and hear you explain that every pick-up coming down the highway is suspicious," said Bonnie, he ignored her and continued to walk around the truck bed to the duffle bag.

"The bag is full of coal," said Bonnie as she slowly followed him, he got to the bag and stopped, waiting. Bonnie stepped over, unsnapped the strap on the bag and folded the flap back exposing the coal. The officer stepped over and ran his hand down the bag, pressing the coal under the fabric, satisfied he stepped back, "who is that," he ask indicating Neil in the truck.

"O.K., that's it, you either write me a ticket or place me under arrest so I can call my lawyer.

The officer ignored her and turned to Neil, Neil had his window open listening to the conversation. "You want to step out of the truck?" As he said this the officer removed his sun glasses and held them in his right hand, his left hand still held the license and registration. Bonnie stood there fuming.

Neil open his door and turned to step out, he looked up and his eyes met the officer's, they were locked in a stare for a full minute.., Bonnie was busy closing the duffle bag, Neil reached down and gently took the license and registration out of the officers hand, he turned to Bonnie and indicated for her to go, without thinking Bonnie raced around the truck bed, got into the drivers seat, Neil closed his window, looked over and said very softly, "let's go," Bonnie fired the engine and looking over her shoulder, pulled onto the hard top and pressed the gas picking up speed, Neil sat there watching the police officer in the side mirror until he was just a speck on the highway. He turned to Bonnie and said, "he'll stand there for a couple more minutes and then put his sunglasses on and walk back to his police car trying to remember what he was standing out there for, In twenty minutes he will have forgotten the whole thing, lucky for us he is very intelligent, it's a learning process and the more intelligent he is the better it works.

Bonnie continue to glance in the rearview mirror and watch the highway until the police officer became a small speck, "he knew better then that," she said, still fuming, "these younger officers have no idea how to handle the power that badge gives them, they do that and in the end they alienate the people who support them the most."

"He has a dangerous job," said Neil.

"Yes he does, but that behavior reflects on every police officer everywhere," Bonnie explained.

She was beginning to relax, she looked over grinning, "is Neil Conrad your real name?"

Neil grinned back at her, "Yes it's my earth name, my legal name you would not be able to pronounce, 'Zwerk Sveragan,' it means morning light or first light."

Bonnie smiled, you are right about the police officer, I tend to let my emotions get the better of me in a situation like that, She explained.

They were in the open desert now, Bonnie was driving over on the edge of the right lane, keeping her speed down so they could talk, "can everybody where you come from do that," she nodded towards the rear of the truck.

"Yes and no, it's a form of advance hypnosis, it's like the martial arts, you have to learn it and in order to be good at it you have to practice it constantly, The Exploration Corps teaches it, it's our first line of defense," he explained.

"You are very good at it," She said.

"Thanks, I thought I was going to have a problem at first with those dark sunglasses but he removed them just at the right moment.

The conversation died away from the noise in the cab and Neil settled back and Bonnie brought the truck up to the speed limit.

The desert stretch off on each side of the highway, to the south were the low purple grey mountains again and the highway continued on to the west.

Bonnie had the pickup a few miles over the speed limit, they sped across the monotony of the desert each with their own thoughts, traffic was light, most of it in the opposite lane going east.

"We are getting close to the truck stop, there is one more thing I have to do," he said, raising his voice over the noise in the cab.

Bonnie took her foot off the gas pedal and let the truck slow to minimum speed, she looked over at him.

"When I left my ship, I had to find clothes, I had no money and I took these and I need to pay for them," he explained.

Bonnie looked over at him grinning, "you mean you..,?" Bonnie ask.

"Yes remember the first rule of the Corps, I expect to leave nothing but finger prints and maybe some DNA behind and that will lead investigators absolutely nowhere," He explained.

Up ahead they could see the buildings of the truck stop breaking the monotony of the desert, "there it is," he said, nodding his head in the direction of the buildings, "just pull over and park in front of the dry goods store."

Bonnie parked and turned the engine off. "We will both go in and I need you to distract the clerk while I put the money on the cash register," as he said this, he took the folded bills from his pocket and began to peel off the bills he needed, he looked at her, "ready?" he ask. She nodded her head.

Bonnie led the way, she stopped at the counter with the cash register and spoke briefly to the clerk and then he turned and led her off to the clothing section, Neil a few paces behind her stopped at the cash register and when he was sure the clerk had his back turned, he placed a hundred dollar bill and three twenties on the cash register and turned and slowly walked back to the truck. Bonnie was quickly in the seat next to him he turned to her and said, "turn back and drive a few miles make a U-turn and come back."

Bonnie backed the truck out, looking over her shoulder as she pulled onto the highway and brought the truck up to minimum speed. She settled back in her seat and glanced over at him, "you know you didn't have to take that risk back there, he would just write the cost of the clothing off."

"I know," he said looking over at her, "but I did that for myself as much as for him.., when we are taught ethics on my planet, there are three things you do not do, you do not lie, cheat or steal. Of the three lying is the big one, a lie is a betrayal, the person who is being lied to is being betrayed.., and cheating, cheating is a lie. Stealing, what can you say about a thief, I think there are countries here on earth that cut off the hand of a person caught stealing.., let me see if I can explain what I did back there this way, lets say there is a box in your conscious and every time you do something wrong, something you know is wrong, a chit is put in the box and this means everything you know to be wrong from spitting gum on the sidewalk all the way up to betraying a friend and even murder, chits are put in the box to the degree of the bad deed and once the chits are put into the box they stay there even as time passes and you forget about the bad deed, the chit is still in the box and as the box gets full you start to make mistakes and the more chits in the box the more mistakes you make until lets say on a beautiful clear day like today, the police come upon an accident where a car has been running full throttle down the highway and the driver suddenly turns and drives into a bridge abutment, the driver is killed, there are no skid marks or indications the brakes were used, the driver just turns right into the abutment, now conscious is not the absolute cause for this every time but there is a good chance it is and after the box is almost full it's possible to start to empty it with good deeds but it's very difficult and once the box is full it's impossible to ignore it.

Bonnie sat with both hands on the steering wheel, eyes on the highway thinking, she turns and glances at him, "what about a couple having sex, a couple making love without marriage?"

Neil took a moment to answer and then said, "I believe it's alright, God gave us sex to procreate but also to enjoy, it's to much fun not to enjoy, if God gave us sex just for procreation, we would be like the animals, there would be no joy and as long as there is responsibility and no lies, I believe it's O.K.., the key to the whole thing is education, especially education in the biology of it. Out of wedlock pregnancy is usually a tragedy for all concerned and it usually is the result of ignorance or irresponsibility or a combination of both, it has been said sex is wasted on youth, it's true, immature sex leads to rejection and once a party has been rejected, they turn to the most vulnerable, Kids and young people and I don't have to elaborate on that."

"The key to the whole thing is maturity and education." He added.

"Then you believe in God?" Bonnie ask.

"Oh yes, something has got to be in control of all of this," he answered.

There was more silence and then he looked over and said' "this is far enough, why don't you look for a place to turn around, make a U-turn and go back to the truck stop."

Bonnie took her foot off the gas and glanced in the rear view mirror as she looked for a place to drive across the medium. She found a spot, slowed and pulled off the hardtop, crossed over to the opposite lanes and turned west, heading back to the truck stop.

"This may not keep the attention off us but I think it is better then just driving across the highway up at the truck stop and parking," Neil said as Bonnie brought the truck up to minimum speed They drove in silence and then Neil spoke.

"Bonnie don't talk about this to anyone.., they wont believe you and they wont believe you because they don't want to, they will come up with many ways you could have gotten the money and without more proof they will not believe you." he said and then he paused, "give me your purse," he said, he began to take the money out of the bag and put it in the purse, he reached into his pocket and pulled out the folded bills and put that in the purse, Bonnie sat looking at the highway and glancing over at him.

He handed her the purse and looked at her, "Bonnie go to Los Angeles and find your agent and become an actress, it wont be easy because there is a lot of competition but you can do it, Use the money for the things you need," He was silent for a moment and then said, "this bag," he indicated the bag between his feet, "has traces of narcotics in it, not enough to convict you of anything but if authorities test it they could give you a lot of aggravation over it, so I will take it with me, the money will have traces also but money with traces of narcotics is probably not that uncommon this close to the border."

They were back at the truck stop, Bonnie was slowing down, Neil looked up and said, "pull up to that scrub brush and park," he pointed ahead, Bonnie did as he said, the truck was about a foot off the hardtop and right across from the fuel island.

After Bonnie turned the engine off, she looked over at him, he had his head down and he appeared to be in deep thought.

He was already in the mental count down for getting back to the ship.

"But what about us, I think I am falling in love with you," Bonnie said.

Neil's head came up and he looked at her for a moment then he reached down and released both seat belts and pulled her close to him and kissed her very deeply, he continued to hold her close and he whispered in her ear, "Bonnie I think I am in love with you too and I have been turning my mind inside out trying to find a way for us, I can not stay here on earth and I can not take you back to the mother ship, I've been dedicated to the Exploration Corps for a very long time and I would have to leave you on the Mother ship, alone for long periods of time and there is the language barrier and you might not like it and there would be no way back at least not for a long time."

"Bonnie," he continued, "none of this can just be luck or coincident, our finding the money and buying the coal and the hotel and the police officer..,

maybe God will put us together again in another time until then when you go out at night I want you to look up at the stars and you will know I am up there somewhere and I will be thinking of you and remembering our love," he kissed her again and said, "I must go," he opened his door and turned back for the bag, "Wait," said Bonnie, "here take my cell phone it has my number in case you cain't get away or you need to call me, I'll be at the ranch."

He took the cell and slid it into his pocket, turned and put the duffle on his right shoulder and taking the bag in his left hand he began walking fast to the brush, at the brush he turned and began to jog into the open desert, he could feel her eyes on his back but he did not turn or look back,

his mind was on the coordinates for the ship and the azimuth he must take to get there, he veered around the brush and picked up his pace until he was running flat out into the open desert.

Bonnie sat watching him as he grew smaller and smaller and then she got out of the cab and climbed up into the truck bed and stood watching him until he disappeared and she continued watching after he was gone and she suddenly realized if he did call she would have to be at the ranch to receive the call. She climbed back down into the cab, started the engine and pulled out onto the highway heading west to the ranch.

It's two weeks later a four wheel drive jeep is winding it's way across the desert, border patrol is lettered on the hood and side of the vehicle they are out there looking for possible lost border crossers, they come to a large circle of disturbed desert, it looks like a large dust devil has started there or touched down in the desert heat, the jeep drives across it and comes to a second one and just as they reach the other side, the vehicle stops and the passenger side door opens, an officer gets out and walks over to a clump of desert growth, he bends over and picks up an old crumpled duffle bag, he carries it back to the hood of the jeep and opens it, he spreads the contents on the hood, a pair of jeans, a dress shirt, belt, an almost new pair of walking shoes, socks and underwear. The officer notices the fine black dust, he rubs it between his fingers and holds it up to his nose, he puts the contents back in the bag and puts the bag in the back of the jeep, gets back in the passenger seat and looks at the driver and says, "we'll take it back to the station and see if we can connect it to anything, it has some kind of fine dust in it, I think it's coal dust."

It has been six weeks since Bonnie stood in the pickup truck bed and watch Neil disappear in the desert with the duffle bag on his shoulder.

The ranch house has a patio on the back facing south. To the west low clouds on the horizon are offering a fine sunset, to the east shadows are gathering for the coming darkness.

Bonnie sits on a lounge chair facing south, she has a small table on her right that has an almost empty glass of ice tea and next to that is her new cell phone, it has not been out of her reach since she watched Neil disappear in the desert. When she bought the new phone she insisted it have the same number as her old phone and although logic tells her Neil has gone and she will probably never see or hear from him again, her heart tells her different, she can not get over the hours and the night they spent together.

Bonnie sits waiting for her father and brother to come in from the ranch, she has planned and prepared the dinner and all that's needed is to put it together and saut'e the chicken, she is waiting to hear their truck, suddenly the cell phone rings.

Bonnie picks up the phone pushes the on button and puts it to her ear all in one motion.

"Hello?"

"Hello.., Bonnie? It's Neil."

Bonnie sat up straight, both feet flat on the floor, "What? Neil where are you?"

"I'm right above you, almost directly overhead..," said Neil.

Bonnie's head went back instinctively and she was staring at the ceiling, she got out of her chair and walked through the screen door and began to search the sky as she held the cell phone to her ear.

"You can't see me, I'm to high but even if I were lower you still would not be able to see me.., how have you been?"

"Oh fine.., I'm fine but how are you? I have been so depressed I would never see you again." Bonnie held the phone to her ear as she walked in an excited circle peering at the sky as if she would suddenly see him appear.

"I have been very busy, I didn't think I would be back but.., well it's a long story we can talk about it later, right now I have got to get down, do you see that high ground to your southeast, I believe you call it a Butte."

"Yes, yes, I see it," Bonnie answered without looking, she knew exactly what he was talking about.

"O.K. there is an unimproved road coming off the interstate and it runs over close to the Butte."

"Yes, yes I know where it is," Bonnie answered still with excitement in her voice.

"O.K., can you meet me there on the road where it comes closes to the Butte at first light in the morning?"

"Yes, yes, I can do that," Bonnie answered still excited and peering up at the sky.

"Oh and can you bring me some jeans and a shirt?"

"Yes my brother is about your size, I'll borrow his," answered Bonnie.

"O.K. sweetheart, well I'm about to become very busy so I'm going to have to hang up now and I will see you in the morning."

"Yes, yes, I love you." I love you too, "said Neil, Bonnie heard the click when they were disconnected but she still stood with the phone to her ear peering up at the empty sky.

Suddenly she pushed the off button on her phone, her mind racing, for the past six weeks she had thought of little else but him and at the same time she was depressed at the thought she would never see him again and now here he was, her mind busy, she walked into the house planing where to start and then she heard the truck with her father and brother, she decided to finish making the dinner first.

As they were eating the dinner Bonnie casually mentioned to her brother she needed to borrow a pair of jeans and a shirt.

"Are you planning on doing some ranch work?" he ask out of curiosity.

"No.., I need to do something, it's complicated, I'll explain later," she said.

"Sure help your self," he answered as she began to clear the table.

Her father noticed how animated and enthusiastic she had become but he said nothing.

The next morning before first light she was turning off the interstate onto the unimproved road leading over to the Butte to her southeast. It had been a clear sky all night and there was a crescent moon with Venus rising to the east and Mars was above and to the right.

As she concentrated on the pot holes of the road, the eastern horizon suddenly began To pale with the new day and then she saw him a figure in the headlights standing on the side of the road.

She slowed and came to stop next to him, she jumped out and ran around the truck and jumped into his arms and they kissed again and again, between kisses they tried to talk, "I've missed you so.., I thought I would never see you again..." Suddenly he held her shoulders and said, "Come on we have got to get out of here before we attract somebodies attention,

did you bring the jeans and shirt?" "Yes," she said as she turned and got back into the truck.

He stood next to the truck bed and pulled off the grey-silver flight suit and put on the jeans and shirt, he turned and got into the passenger side of the truck cab. He leaned over and kissed her again and said, "can we make it without the lights, we cain't have anybody snooping around the Butte, the ship is invisible but somebody could stumble upon it."

"Sure," said Bonnie she reached down and turned off the lights. The desert growth grew right up to the edge of the road on each side and the eastern horizon was changing from from grey to sky blue and the days new light illuminated the road enough to drive. She looked at him as he neatly folded the flight suit, "you can fit it behind the seat," he looked at her and smiled.

"Those are nice looking shoes," she said looking down at his feet.

"Yes they are new from my planet," he began to explain, "They shed dirt and water, they breath, they wear like iron and they are as comfortable as walking on air, I figure I will wear them until we can find some more."

"Yes, I don't think they will be noticed, they fit right in."

"Well let's see, 'oh', have you had breakfast?" Bonny asked.

"No, how about you?"

"No, we can stop up here and get some."

They reached the divided highway and Bonnie stopped and checked if she was clear and pulled out onto the highway heading west.

Bonnie closed her window and reached down and turned on the air conditioner, He rolled up his window as Bonnie picked up speed.

"There is a small town just down the road, we can have breakfast there,"

said Bonnie, raising her voice over the noise inside the cab.

Neil settled back in the air-conditioning and waited until they could talk without the noise in the cab.

Soon they could make out buildings in the flat desert ahead, "that looks like the place up ahead," said Neil.

"Yes, I've eaten there before it's not bad," said Bonnie. She pulled into the parking lot of a two story building with a small neon sign that flashed OPEN in red. The parking lot was not empty and as they walked into the front door they could see a counter with stools against the far wall and booths lined the other walls on each side. They chose a booth on the right side of the room and sat down.

The waitress brought water and silverware and turned for the coffee as Bonnie and Neil glanced at the menu. The waitress returned with coffee and took their orders.

Bonnie sat looking into Neil's eyes, she wore a contented smile of admiration, Neil returned her smile and reached across the table and took her hands in his.

"So how have you been?" Bonnie ask.

"Good, good," said Neil smiling in her eyes.

"I've spent most of the past six weeks going and coming, I never realized how boring and long those missions were until I had to leave you."

Bonnie sat looking into his eyes taking in every word.

Neil continued, "when I got there I turned in my report and while I waited for a response, I learned they picked up a message from that sinister force I spoke of earlier and it seems the force found a planet in a solar system where the people were still in the stone age, about to move into the bronze age, the sinister force introduced a virus and just left, they'll return in a year or so and take over the planet, by that time the inhabitants should all be dead, and there will be nothing to stop them.

Bonnie, "what will your people do?"

"They'll probably send a mission in there and get rid of the virus.., they were very interested in my report and the fact that we formed a relationship, they are impressed with how compassionate the people on earth are and my mission is to come back here, continue the relationship and give earth as much help as I can to build a spaceship out above low earth orbit and get earth into space travel as soon as possible. My planet wants earth as an ally against the SACHOIDS.., that word translates roughly as baby eaters

The waitress returned with the coffee and Bonnie gave the order for breakfast.

"They gave me some drugs so I can breath earths atmosphere, I have to take a pill each day," said Neil.

"How will we get started," ask Bonnie.

The waitress interrupted with their breakfast.

They began to eat as they smiled into each others eyes.

"The first thing we will have to do is unite all the nations, get them to give up all sectarian wars and come together like some natIons did to build the space station, to build this space ship it will have to be done outside low earth orbit and it will have to be opened to all nations and then we will gather all the best engineers and designers," Neil explained.

"I can help a lot and any problems I can't solve, I can go back to my Headquarters ship and they can send plans and advice," Neil explained between bites.

"Wow it sounds like we have our work cut out for us," said Bonnie.

"Yes well it may not be all that difficult, the first step will be to find a man with a lot of money and power and get him on our side." Neil explained.

"We'll need a computer," Neil continued To explain.

"I brought my lap top, it's in the truck,' said Bonnie.

"Good where is the nearest collection or group of capital?" Neil ask.

"That would be Dallas - Ft Worth or Houston, there is a lot of oil money in Oklahoma but probably Houston Texas would be the place with the most money," Bonnie explains.

"O.K. we will start our search in Houston Texas," said Neil.

They finished breakfast and lingered over the second cup of coffee, Bonnie paid the bill leaving a nice tip and they got back into the truck, Bonnie turned back into the sunrise heading for Houston, Neil had the lap top on his lap and with his knowledge of electronics he soon had the lap top giving him the information he wanted.

The landscape began to change, green plants began to appear on each side of the highway, at first one or two and then more and more and then they crossed the Pecos river and the landscape changed from burnt out desert to green trees and scrubs.

"Have you heard of Crane Industries?" Neil ask without looking up from the laptop.

"Vaguely," said Bonnie, keeping her eyes on the road, it's owned by a man named Raymond Crane, he is supposed to be pretty well off." Bonnie continued.

There were several more miles of silence as a bonnie kept her eyes on the road and Neil tapped on the lap top.

"Well it looks like Raymond Crane is our man," said Neil looking over at Bonnie, "he is into solar energy and he has some wind farms and he is invested in oil, railroads and other things, he is headquartered in

Houston and my guess is he has a large engineering department," his statement trailed off as he looked back at the laptop.

Traffic was beginning to pickup as the day wore on and they got closer to towns, "what do you have in mind?" Bonnie ask keeping her eyes on the road. "He's well diversified in his investments and from what I have read here he will take a risk if there is the possibility of a profit.., if we can get him on our side he could probably influence other people," said Neil, looking up at Bonnie and then back down at the laptop screen.

They continued on for miles in silence, Bonnie glanced over at Neil, "I left a note for my Dad and Brother explaining I would be away for a few days.., we can have lunch in Houston we should be there soon."

"That sounds good," Neil looked up from he laptop screen, "It's interesting how much information is on this laptop and it is pretty easy to use."

"Yes," said Bonnie, "you don't believe that when you first open one but it gets easier after you use it for a while."

The sun was overhead now and the traffic was getting heavier and heavier as they neared the outskirts of Houston. "There is a hotel right across from Crane Industries," said Neil looking up from the computer screen, "we can check in there and have lunch before we try to get an appointment with Raymond Crane."

"Sounds good," said Bonnie, without taking her eyes off the traffic.

They found the parking lot for the hotel and checked in.

Neil carried the laptop in it's case and Bonnie's overnight bag, they took the key and found the room themselves.

Neil set the bags down at the closest spot in the room and turned to Bonnie, taking her in his arms, they kissed and kissed and holding her close Neil whispered, "let me watch you undress and then I would like to take a quick shower."

It was 45 minutes later, they lay on the bed, the sheets pulled back.

Bonnie lay looking at the ceiling, "You know I have been thinking, what we should do is get you a business suit and tie before we meet Mr. Crane."

Neil turned and looked at her, "that sounds like a good idea, how do we go about it?"

"Find a department store or a men's wear store, you should be able to wear one right off the rack as they say," She threw her legs off the bed, "come on let's go see what we can find."

There was a men's wear store right off the lobby, it had a street entrance and an entrance from the lobby. Bonnie explained they had just arrived in town and they needed a new suit as quickly as possible. The store owner was also the tailor, he had a tape measure around his neck and after taking Neil's measurements he began to display an assortment of different colored suits, Bonnie chose a dark blue pin strip and as the clerk began to measure and fit Neil, she moved off and began to choose a matching tie and shirts. The shop owner promised the suit later that afternoon. Bonnie and Neil went in search of a late lunch after Bonnie paid for the suit with her credit card.

They were seated in a better restaurant just down the street from the hotel. Neil sat with a piece of bread in his hand he had taken a bite from, he kept glancing at a man sitting alone in a booth against the wall. Bonnie sat watching him and finally she turned and looked in the direction Neil kept glancing at, "Who are you looking at?" she ask turning back to face him.

"That man there in the booth, he's having some very sinister thoughts," said Neil, as he looked into her eyes.

"Sinister thoughts about what?" Bonnie ask

"Sinister thoughts about hurting someone he knows, even killing them." Neil said.

They were interrupted by the waiter bringing their order, Bonnie ordered two salads for lunch.

Neil starts to explain as they began to eat the salad.

"Mind reading on my planet is pretty much a common thing, the Exploration Corps teach and practice it constantly, it is our first line of defense.., but it's like the martial arts, to be good at it you have to practice it constantly, we are trained to ignore it in public unless we come across something like we have here.

Neil took another bite of salad and his eyes began to wonder across the dinning room settling on the booth the man was in, the man continued to eat his food, slowly chewing and as he finished the food he sat sipping his beverage and his mind went back to what he was thinking about.

Neil looked into Bonnie's eyes, "you can not arrest a man for what he is thinking but he is very definitely plotting how he can get away with the perfect murder."

Bonnie casually glanced in the direction of the booth and focused on the man, he was studying his bill, her eyes came back to Neil's, "there must be something we can do."

Neil took a final bite of the salad and put his fork on the plate, he used his napkin, "no there really isn't, how am I going to explain to the police that I read his mind.., on my planet I could, but not here, not now, we cain't just lock him up forever and then there are the random thoughts and the determined planning, I can tell the difference with my training but I wont be able to explain it."

"I see," said Bonnie.

"All we can do is forget about it and hope something happens that will change the situation," said Neil.

"Wow," said Bonnie, "well I guess sometimes we are better off with what we don't know."

"Yes," said Neil, "well I guess we should start thinking about how we are going to handle the appointment with Mr. Crane.., I can handle it once we make eye contact but we have to get to that point, I think you need to call and make the appointment, a female voice will sound like a secretary making an appointment for her boss."

"I think I can handle that," said Bonnie.

The waitress stopped at the table and ask if they would like desert, "no everything is fine, can we have the bill," ask Bonnie.

Neil watched Bonnie pay the bill and when he looked up again, the man was leaving the booth.., his mind was blank, Neil turned his mind to other things.

They returned to the hotel, the maid had been in and the bed was made and the room was straighten up. They called the taylor shop and had the suit delivered to the room when it was finished. Neil sat watching Bonnie undress and they took advantage of the bed again and then watched the television news. When they went down to dinner the bed was a total mess again.

They sat across from each other in a booth "what will you try to do at Crane Industries?" Bonnie ask.

"I will try to get them to build a new concept in electric motors and a better battery is needed here on earth." After a pause, Neil continued, "earth needs clean energy and a more efficient battery and an electric motor would be the first step.

They finished dinner and started back to the room, the desk clerk motioned for Neil and gave him the suit that had been delivered. They continued to the room, the maid had not been in and the bed was still a mess. They undressed and returned to the bed.

The next morning Neil took a shower first and came out dressed in his new suit, he was trying to tie the new tie Bonnie picked out for him.

Bonnie was hanging up the phone, "I just got us an appointment for this morning," she said this as she walked over and tied his tie for him, she stepped back and admired him, "you look like an investment banker, a very successful investment banker," she smiled.

"Good that's what we need," said Neil.

Bonnie took a quick shower and they went down for breakfast.

They returned to the room to freshen up and then left for Crane Industries looking like two successful business people.

The guard stationed in the lobby directed them to a bank of elevators that took them to the executive offices on the top floor and they were standing before Raymond Crane's secretary's desk at ten sharp.

Bonnie introduced them, the secretary picked up her phone spoke briefly and then stood and led them into an inner office, the secretary tapped gently on the door and then opened it, Bonnie led the way, the light was subdued in the room, the blinds were pulled against the morning sun, the lamp on Raymond's desk was on, giving light to the papers on the desk.

Raymond stood as Bonnie approached the desk and stepped aside for Neil, Raymond walked around his desk extending his hand, "Neil Conrad," said Bonnie as the two men shook hands, Raymond turned to Bonnie after shaking Neil's hand, "Bonnie Steward," said Bonnie as she took his hand.

Raymond Crane walked back around his desk, pausing to pull the cord on the blind, filling the room with the morning light, he indicated

Bonnie and Neil should take the two chairs in front of his desk, everyone settled back.

Raymond Crane was average in high, his light brown hair was thinning and giving way to grey but his body carried little fat and he looked much younger then his years. Bonnie noticed how much more posh the carpet was when she stepped into the room and now with the room lighted, she quickly scanned the room, she noted the paintings on the walls and quickly judged them to be originals, and she noted objet d'art placed about the room that gave testimony to Raymond Crane's affluence and good taste.

Neil paused making eye contact with Raymond as he settled into his chair, then Neil spoke, "Mr. Crane this is a beautiful morning and I don't want to take up too much of your time so I will come right to the point, we are here because of your success in your industry.., I have an idea for a new electric motor and I think Crane Industries is the company that could build a prototype." Neil paused for a moment continuing to make eye contact.

Raymond broke eye contact and settled back in his chair, then he spoke, "engineering new concepts is a large part of what Crane Industries is all about, what kind of motor do you have in mind?"

"We have an idea for a motor that is a little smaller but produces more power and uses less energy then any motor out there," said Neil as he continued to make eye contact.

"That sounds like what we are working on now," said Raymond.

"I wonder, could I have a look at your engineering dept." ask Neil.

"Well yes, I'm sure they are not working on anything that radical, we are just trying to upgrade what we already have.., the engineering department is down on the third floor," Raymond pushed back from his desk as he said this.

As they rode the elevator down to the third floor, Raymond Crane was totally unaware he was under the hypnotic influence of Neil Conrad.

The engineering department office opened to a large room that had computer cubical desks with lighted computers screens, several men worked at the key boards, farther into the room were desk with drawing boards and fluorescence lights lighting the boards. A man was bent over a drawing board.

Bonnie, Neil and Raymond Crane stopped at the front of the room. "Wow this is impressive," said Bonnie.

"Yes," said Raymond, "we try to keep up with the latest engineering thinking and buy the best soft wear."

As Bonnie and Raymond continued to talk, Neil walked into the room to the man who was bent over the drawing board. Neil stood over the man, "Hello do you mind if I look over your shoulder?"

The man turned his head and looked up at Neil, "no not at all, it looks like I have hit a dead end."

Neil stood studying the drawing for a moment, "this is very impressive.., have you thought about this," Neil ripped off a sheet of tracing paper and taped it over the drawing, he picked up a pencil and a straight edge and began to add to the drawing, he finished by leaving a three line note at the bottom of the tracing paper.

Neil stood and backed away as the man pulled his seat back to the drawing board and began studying what Neil put on the drawing. Neil turned and walked back to where Bonnie and Raymond stood talking.

Neil stopped at one of the computer screens, "hello do you mind if I take a look?" The man on the keyboard looked up at him, he pushed his chair back and said, "no not at all."

Neil stood studying the screen for a moment and said, "this is a good idea.., have you thought of this?" Neil learned the key board from Bonnie's lap top and he bent over now and began to hunt and peck on the key board. The keyboard engineer just sat back and watched.

Neil finished and stood up, as he backed away the engineer pulled his chair back and began to study the screen as Neil turned and joined Bonnie and Raymond.

The three walked to the bank of elevators leaving the engineering department abuzz with, "Hey who was that guy?" "Where did he come from..,? And more important where did he go..,?" "He took about two minutes to solve a problem I have been stymied with for a few months..."

The three, Bonnie, Neil and Raymond got on an elevator for the executive offices, "that's a very impressive engineering department," said Neil.

"Thank you," answered Raymond, "I'm very proud of it, we all try to keep abreast of the latest scientific and engineering developments and I buy all the latest soft wear." "The machine shop and construction takes place in another building not far from here, they can build just about anything the engineering department can come up with," Raymond continued to explain.

The elevator door opened at Raymond's office again and the three walked off. Neil stopped at the door of Raymond's office, he turned to Raymond, "Mr. Crane I am impressed with what I've seen here and I don't want an answer now, but if you talk to your legal department about.., if I come in here with an idea for a new electric motor and you build a prototype, how can we set up ownership, copyrights, profits and so on, give me a call and we can get together, we are staying in the 'Wyndly' across the street."

"That's a good idea," said Raymond, "I would like to talk to legal."

Bonnie and Neil turned back to the elevator and Raymond was not settled in his office chair good before he began to hear stories from the engineering department about Neil's brief visit.

"Who was that?" "Where did he come from?" "Yeah who was that guy and where did he go, in two minutes he solved a problem that has had me stymied for months." The buzzing continued and Raymond had to take this to the legal department and talk to them about taking on a new concept in electric motors.

It was a little after nine the next morning, Bonnie and Neil were retuning from breakfast, the desk clerk motioned them over, a message from Raymond Crane, "could they meet in his office after ten?"

Bonnie and Neil continued on to their room, freshened up and then walked across the street to Raymond's office. The secretary ushered them into Raymond's office, he stood, walked around his desk with his right hand extended, he was smiling, he got them seated, would you like coffee, tea?

He ask as he returned to his seat? Bonnie looked at Neil then said "no, we are good."

"Well you certainly impressed my engineering department yesterday, with the help you have given them they are already on their way to greatly improving our electric motor," said Raymond.

"That's fine," said Neil," "but you know I think with the time it would take to redesign the old motor and rebuild it, we could design a completely new concept, design it and build a prototype.

Raymond was slightly taken aback, he sat back in his chair, "are you sure..,? Many things can go wrong with a project like that," Raymond questioned.

"Oh yes," answered Neil, "I've seen motors similar to the one I have in mind and they work just fine,"

Raymond paused a moment thinking.., "alright then, a completely new design..," after a pause he began thinking ahead, "alright you will be in charge, we will do the designing here and as soon as the plans are ready we can take them over to the factory and build it." this will all have to be hush-hush until we are ready," he looked at Bonnie, "when we are ready we will need a big public relation campaign, I looked at your background," he said, then paused and continued to look at Bonnie, then he spoke, "I think you would be good to head up the PR campaign for this."

"Well that is an interesting thought," Bonnie said and then paused.

"Well there is plenty of time for that, right now we need to get busy with the design," Raymond turned back to Neil, "I've talked to legal as I said and this is what they propose, you two will be on salary until the prototype is finished and then there will be a nice bonus." Raymond stopped there and let what he said sink in..," and then he continued, "this of course depends on the prototype working, that the prototype is a success."

Raymond paused again and looked at Bonnie and Neil and watched them nod in agreement.

"O.K. then," said Raymond, "Neil I have briefed the engineering department on this and they are expecting you down there, so I put the engineering department at your disposal, you can start clean."

"Well that's fine, with a clean sheet of paper and the cooperation of your people I am sure we can give you a radical new prototype," said Neil.

"Good," said Raymond as he stood at his desk, "and while you are down there getting organized, I want to take this lady down to advertising and show her what we have."

With that both Bonnie and Neil stood and they walked to the elevator.

At the sixth floor the elevator stopped, Raymond looked at Neil and said,

"Ride down to the third floor, they are expecting you, they are expecting you to upgrade the existing engine, I'll let you fill them in on the radical new design."

"That's fine," said Neil, stepping back from the door, he smiled at Bonnie and said, "I'll catch you later."

Raymond finally had Bonnie alone and as they walked down the hallway towards a sign that read advertising department, Raymond turned and glanced at Bonnie, "Bonnie, as I said, I looked into your background and I liked what I saw, but I also tried to look into Neil's background and I came up with a big blank, there is absolutely nothing past yesterday morning.., who is he.., ?" Where did he come from..,? ""Where did he learn so much about engineering and energy production?"

Bonnie took several more steps in silence and then she stopped and backed against the wall, she looked Raymond in the eye, "he's not from here."

Raymond looked in her eyes and said, "yes I know, but where.., where is he from?"

Bonnie continued to look into his eyes and said, "he is from the other end of the galaxy.., he's from outer space."

"What!" said Raymond.

"He's from another planet he's just visiting here," Bonnie said unsure of herself.

Raymond stood there in silence, finally he spoke, "well I can believe that..,

in five minutes he gave the engineering department information that is just not available, I noticed he seemed a bit different .., well we need to talk about this, we need to sit down, let's go back to the office," he turned and they walked back to the elevator.

They were both comfortably seated in Raymond's office and Bonnie decided she could trust this man and she began to give him the full story, she began at the fuel stop where they first met, he told me he was 123 years old by earth's standards, He said his life's expectancy was two hundred years on his planet," Raymond Crane sat giving her his full attention.

"Well yes.., I can believe that," said Raymond, "in talking with him he had a certain air about him, in talking with him you felt he could answer just about any question you could ask and offer a solution to just about any problem...

Finally Bonnie concluded with their visit here at the office.

"Well this puts a different slant on things," said Raymond, there was silence as he began to think.

Up near the top of the building on the nineteenth floor the company had a cafeteria, they had a creditable chef and a separate executive dinning room, Raymond entertained special guest and customers there.

Raymond looked at his watch, then he looked at Bonnie, "it's almost lunch time, go down to engineering and bring Neil up to the nineteenth floor, we have a cafeteria there, someone will guide you to the executive dining room, I've got to make some phone calls..,"

"Huh.., he doesn't want this known, that is, who he is, I've probably told you to much already," said Bonnie.

"No, no, it's alright, I've got to cancel some appointments," said Raymond, "meet me there in about thirty minutes." he picked up his phone, Bonnie stood turned and walked to the elevator, the engineering department was busy with activity as Bonnie entered, she looked around and saw Neil at the far side of the room, he was standing over a man that was hunched over a lighted drawing board, he sensed Bonnie's presence, he turned and saw her walking towards him, "I've come to take you to lunch,"

said Bonnie.

Neil turned and looked around him, "O.K. well I think they have enough to keep them busy for a while so lunch it is," They turned and walked to the elevator. Bonnie waited until the elevator door was closed and they were on their way to the nineteenth floor.

She turned and looked into Neil's eyes, "I had to tell him who you were."

"Huh-O," said Neil.

"No it's alright, he's very excited," said Bonnie as the elevator door opened.

The cafeteria was impressive, a man in a white jacket approached, Bonnie introduced them and he led them to the executive dinning room that was even more impressive, They were seated at a corner table with a breath catching view of the south side of the city, Bonnie looked at Neil, "he tried to look into your background and there was nothing there, I had to tell him."

"It's O.K.," said Neil as he looked up and saw Raymond enter the dinning room.

Once they were all seated, Raymond said, "I had to cancel some appointments I had with friends and business colleagues," he paused a moment then continued, "I'm pretty sure this table and corner is secure, free of any bugs that is, but with todays technology you can never be certain."

Raymond leaned back in his chair and looked at Neil, taking him in, in a different light. "Bonnie tells me you are a visitor to our planet, a visitor from outer space."

He stopped speaking, there was a moment of silence.

"Yes, yes that is true," said Neil.

"Well," said Raymond, "I've got about a million questions, let me start with how did you get here?"

"The first time I made an emergency landing near Bonnie's ranch and the second time I just landed on an obscure butte near her place and speaking of that, I am becoming concerned about the ship, it's invisible but someone could stumble upon it and that would not be good."

"Yes, I understand," said Raymond, "how big is the ship?"

"It's a little bigger then your more advanced fighters, it would fit into your average hanger," said Neil.

"O.K.," said Raymond, there is an old Army air field on the south side of the city, it was built during WWII but the army has long since abandoned it and it has become a field for private aircraft, I have just renovated a hanger there, I was planning on using the field for our corporate aircraft, you could fly in during the early morning hours when there are few people around, there is a control tower but it gets pretty quite after midnight and I can guarantee 24 hours security."

The waiter interrupted giving everyone a menu, Bonnie ask for ice tea and Neil and then Raymond nodded also.

"Actually my ship lands like a helicopter so if most of the lights are off except for a landing area there won't be much to see," said Neil.

"What about the electric motor, what will it do?" Ask Raymond.

"It will be a little smaller then your top of the line motor but it will have a lot more horsepower, the most radical thing about it will be, it's wired differently and it's made of different kinds of material, but the real thing about it will be the alternator, the alternator will be much like the alternators on your internal combustion engines only it will be much more sophisticated, it will have two banks of batteries, the engine will run on one bank and as the batteries are depleted, the alternator will switch it to the fresh batteries and then recharge the original battery." Neil explained.

"Wow do you think it will work?" said Raymond.

"Oh sure, it's pretty routine for my planet and we will have to redesign the lithium batteries but it's not perpetual motion, you have to stop every twelve to fifteen hundred miles and give both battery packs a slow charge but it's clean and efficient," said Neil.

"Wow again," said Raymond, "this is the kind of thing I've been trying to get out my engineering department for months, years even, this will certainly begin to change everything."

"Yes it will," said Neil. "and that is the reason we have to keep all this a secret until we are ready. We need to build the prototype, put it in a truck, send it over to the east coast bring it back here, evaluate it and if everything checks out, send it to the west coast and bring it back here and if everything is O.K. we can talk to the media, what we don't need is the media jumping all over every problem we my have, if everything works well, we can let Bonnie here have a media event."

"I can see you have thought this through, that's good," said Raymond.

"Thank you," said Neil, "but engineering is not the real problem we have, the real problem is diplomacy, I don't know how much Bonnie has told you but we have got to build a space ship outside low earth orbit, a spaceship that is capable of journeying outside this solar system, to other solar systems to other worlds and this will take the cooperation of all the nations on earth." "the United Nations is a start but we have got to convince all Nations on earth to give up their internecine wars and conflicts and cooperate towards this common goal."

"Yes and that will take some diplomacy alright," said Raymond.

"The reason we picked you is because of your power and influence.., we assumed you would have friends in the same position and you could persuade them to see this in the same way," explained Neil.

"Yes I see your point," said Raymond.

There was silence as everyone considered what had just been said.

"Your technology is really advancing now and what we want to do here on your planet is advance the technology about seven hundred to one thousand years more," Neil spoke in the silence, "but it will not be easy, you've done a good job with atomic energy over the past sixty years or so, but there are signs it may be coming apart and that is not your only problem, I see your real problem is over population, you are already destroying forest that make your oxygen in order to produce food and you can not win that, the ever increasing population will out run your ability to feed it..."

"Yes and some of us are concerned about climate change" Raymond added.

"Well climate change is an on going thing and it can be handled with technology, with such things as drought resistant crops and so on..," said Neil. "The real problem is overpopulation, if the population increase continues, the working class will get to the point they can not afford to buy the better food and this will lead to malnutrition and starvation and it will bring on disease and plagues."

"Yes I've seen the quality of life on this planet deteriorate in my lifetime," said Bonnie.

This got a nod from Raymond .., Then Neil repeated, "We need to quietly build the electric motor, put it in a semi truck and run it over to the east coast and back and if everything works we can then continue on to the west coast and back, when we get it back here we can have a media event as they say but we need to keep it quiet until we make a coast to coast run with it and if we have a problem we wont need the media jumping all over it."

Raymond leaned back in his chair, "that sounds like a good idea but then what?"

"Well if Bonnie does a public relations job and gives it to the media, it should make headlines," said Neil, what happens then is the petroleum industries will be up in arms and that is where your influence comes in, if you have enough power and influence to counter the petroleum industries we can move on to bigger things like high speed rail and influencing the U. N. and the other Nations to join in an effort to build an earth spaceship."

They were interrupted by the waiter taking the orders.

Raymond squeezed his lemon then sweetened his tea, he took a sip and said, "high speed rail, now that is something I have been thinking about, but that is going to take a lot of money."

"Yes it will," said Neil, "but if it's done right, if we build a high speed rail system on the right of way of your present rail system it should hold the cost down and if you hold the patent on a radical new power system it will give you leverage."

The waiter began to bring the food and the conversation trailed off.

The waiter left and Raymond picked up his fork, took a bite and used his napkin, "it looks like the new electric motor will be the key to the whole thing."

"It will be the start," said Neil, "your Hubble space telescope has shown a little of what's out there and your Kepler space telescope, looking for exoplanets, at the latest count has found two planets in the Cinderella zone as they are called, not too close to it's star and not to far away, so that water stays liquid and so forth, they are similar to earth, one is twenty light years away from earth and the other is six..,"

Raymond interrupts, "light years?"

"Yes," said Neil, "the time it takes to reach a point at the speed of light."

"Well I Know there is nothing on planet earth that is anywhere near that,"

comments Raymond.

"My headquarters ship is capable of speeds like that, but it takes a lot of energy, we are working on that now, trying to get the engines to sustain that speed using less fuel," said Neil, then he continued, "the reason you have to build your space ship outside low earth orbit, you will need outer space to test the engines, you can test the theory of the engines on earth but to test the engines you need outer space."

Although they continued to nibble at the food, Neil had Raymond Crane's complete attention.

"Your newest telescope the J.W.S.T., the James Webb Space Telescope will find other planets like earth and within ten years you will be communicating with them and when that happens you have to be ready."

Raymond sat looking at Neil with a puzzled and incredulous look on his face.

"Electric motors or solar-electric propulsion is probably the answer, everyone is using and thinking chemical engines now but chemical propulsion is so heavy and heavy means cost, cost to get it out there and maintain it.

Solar-electric propulsion is slow but it's lightweight and less costly," said Neil, "your Mars rover is running on electric power generated by Pu-238 pellets left over from your cold war and the supply is limited and just throwing money at the problem will not fix it. it will take time, the answer my be to generate more speed with electric or solar-electric propulsion."

Neil paused, took several bites and continued, "As I said, I came from the other end of the galaxy, this is our first attempt at exploring this part of the galaxy and while I was on my way here and crashed landed, the Headquarters Ship came across our main adversaries the Sachoids."

"That word translates into English as approximately, "baby eaters" or 'the infant eaters...,' we have never confronted the Sachoids or fought them in any way, we have picked up their messages and we have been just where they left and frankly it is not very pretty," explained Neil.

"Your English is very good, in fact just hearing your English makes it hard to believe you are not from here," said Raymond. "Thank you, as I've said to Bonnie, one thing about space travel, you have plenty of time on your hands, we've been studying Planet Earth for some time now and I have been studying English since we first picked it up on the airwaves and since landing here, I have really studied it," said Neil.

"Well you have become very good at it," said Raymond.

"Thanks, I have a talent for it, a musical ear I believe you call it," said Neil.

There was a pause as they continued to eat.

Raymond took a bite, put his knife and fork down and used his napkin, "so let me repeat this to get it straight, your planet, your people want to help us so we can become allies against the other force, what did you call them? Sachoids?"

"Yes simple said that's about it, "Neil said,' my Headquarters Ship is over at another solar system where the Sachoids introduced a deadly virus, the Sachoids will come back in about a year or so and if there are any survivors among the Hunters and Gatherers, the Sachoids will just kill them off and take over the planet's natural resources, we have seen other planet where they have been and they are a blood thirsty bunch and as I have said we have not engaged them or confronted them in any way so we do not know what kind of weapons they have or what they are capable of."

"Mmm, well I can see the need for allies," said Raymond as he picked up his fork.

"To build a spaceship that is capable of intergalactic travel will take more then throwing money at it as you say," Neil began to explain.., "a two year trip to Mars for instance will expose the crew to a lethal dose of space radiation and the farther away from the earth and the sun you move the more radiation you will be exposed to. The spaceship will need protection from high-energy atomic particles flying around in open space once you get past the magnetic fields of earth so you need the cooperation of everyone on earth.., I am constantly amazed at where original and very competent ideas come from."

"So you are saying we need the cooperation of all the nations on earth plus the input from these nations," said Raymond.

"Yes they will all willingly give to the cause once it is made clear to them how important it is." said Neil.

Raymond used his napkin, laid it on the table edge and looked at his watch, "this gives me a multitude of things to think about and do.., what? How are you going to get back to the ship?"

"We have a pick-up truck from the ranch," said Bonnie.

"A pick-up truck?" "Go down to the company motor pool, leave the truck there and take a company car, it will be more comfortable and probably faster, I'll call down and tell them you are coming," said Raymond.

"Oh well that 's very generous of you," Bonnie said, "but we have a lot of unimproved roads to travel on and the pick-up is more suitable for that, even though a sedan would be more comfortable."

After a pause, Raymond said, "stop by the airport and check out your landing spot, I'll call my man and tell him you are coming," with that said Raymond pushed his chair back, stood and left the dinning room, as he walked to the elevator his mind was full of questions, he knew now Crane Industries would not have exclusive ownership and copyrights to the electric motor and he would not have exclusive rights to profits but that was alright there would be profit enough being the source of all this and then there was his high-speed rail system, he would have a hard time waiting for the prototype of the new electric motor, he stepped off the elevator and hurried to his office.

Bonnie and Neil finished their lunch, Bonnie looked up and said, "we may as well go and check out of the hotel, we can check with the desk downstairs and find out where the company motor pool is."

Neil looked up and nodded as he pushed back from the table and they left the dinning room, the waiter was standing near the entrance, Neil paused and told him how good the lunch was, they stopped at the lobby and checked with the reception desk and were told the motor pool was the first two floors of the parking lot building, a block down the street.

They returned to the hotel, the maid had been in and straightened up the room, she made the bed. Neil changed out of his suit and began to put on his blue jeans, he looked up at Bonnie, she was smiling at him...

Bonnie finally packed the bags and when they left the room the bed was a big mess again.

They took the pick-up from the hotel parking lot and stopped by the motor pool at Crane industries, Bonnie got directions to the airport and Crane aviation's hanger from the parking lot attendant, they both settled into the familiar comfort of the pick-up, Bonnie looked over and said, "are you ready?" "Yes ma'am .., proceed."

Neil stood in front of the hanger door, Raymond's aviation man stood next to him, Neil took several steps away and turned a complete circle slowly orientating himself with the area, he noted where the control tower was and the main runway, he stepped back to where the aviation man was and pointed out a big circle where he wanted landing lights and then warned the man to be prepared for a big helicopter down wash and make sure there was nothing in the circle, no vehicles, no people, nothing. The man assured him everything would be ready and he had alerted the control tower the ship would be coming in here in the early morning hours. Neil told him he would call the tower and the only thing they would see in the darkness would be one landing light. With that, Bonnie and Neil got back into the pick-up and Bonnie turned for the Highway heading up to I-10 and then west to the ranch and the ship. She had to watch her speed because with the pick-up out there away from the traffic of the city, it just did not seem she was going that fast, she settled back. Neil sat with her lap-top on his lap, tapping away.

"Look out ! "He's not going to stop," Neil shouts, another pick-up, on a road that intersects the highway they are on, comes to the intersection and turns right into them. Bonnie hits the brakes, leaving rubber on the asphalt but there is not enough room, her pick-up smashes right into the other truck.

Nobody is injured but Bonnie's truck is totally disabled, the traffic police are called, Bonnie's truck is towed, the insurance covers it and her and She and Neil get a rental car and continue the trip.

Bonnie and Neil are in the rental car, Neil sits with the lap-top, he looks over at Bonnie, "well that settles it, something has got to be done about all the automobiles on the roads."

"I agree, I cain't imagine what that driver was thinking." said Bonnie.

"Well that's the point, he wasn't thinking, to pull out like that." said Neil.

The sun had set as they reached the unimproved road leading off into the desert. Neil closed the lap-top as Bonnie began to steer among the pot holes and ruts. The light faded fast as they moved past the desert growth Neil looked over and said, "don't turn on the lights until you have to."

Bonnie looked over at him, "I'll have to soon." "It's right up here," Neil nodded his head forward as he said this, then he pushed his seat all the way back, turned and put the lap-top on the back seat and took the flight suit they brought and began the intricate maneuver of changing from jeans and long sleeve shirt to the flight suit. He looked at Bonnie when he had the flight suit on and then looked around at the desert,

"This is good stop here," he pulled a cell phone size instrument out and began to push buttons, "everything at the ship is fine," he said as he put the instrument away.

He turned to Bonnie and said, "when I get on board, I'll contact the headquarters and report in, it will be several hours before I take off and even if there was light you would not see anything but a cloud of dust, so go on to the ranch and go to bed, drive back to Houston in the morning, I'll meet you at the airport," with that said he reached over and took her in his arms. They kissed and whispered into each others ears and kissed again finally Neil pulled back and said, "give me a couple of minutes before you turn on the lights," with that he turned and stepped into the desert sand wearing the new shoes from his planet, he turned back and said, "be careful driving," and he disappeared into the desert darkness.

There was a new moon and it was pitch black in the desert, Bonnie checked her watch and after five minutes she started the pick-up and turned on the low beam lights and slowly drove down the dirt road to I-10 and then back to the ranch.

Bonnie's father and brother had finished their dinner and gathered in the kitchen and talked while Bonnie made herself a sandwich from left over steak, She told her family she had a great job with Crane Industries and she had a new rental car outside and the pick-up was in Houston, she was careful not to talk about Neil. She was tired after the long drive and she went to bed early.

Bonnie woke early at least two hours before first light, she slipped into the kitchen made a cup of coffee and had a bowl of cold cereal, she wrote a note for her father and brother, packed a bag and slipped out of the house and was on the road driving into the morning sun.

Neil reached the ship and began the preflight checking, he composed and sent a message to the headquarters ship, it would take hours to get there and he would probably be in Houston when the message arrived. He took a quick nap as he waited and then at about the time Bonnie woke, he lifted off the butte for the twenty minute slow run to Houston, his radar kept him aware of all aircraft in the area and he picked up the lights of Houston. He called the tower at the field and told them he was landing at the Crane Industries hanger, he turned final and turned on the single landing light on the bottom of the ship then picked up the circle of lights at the hanger, he came down in a blast from the engines and when the wheels touched he shut down the engine.

The Crane Industries Aviation man stepped out of a small door and walked towards the ship, Neil was just climbing down from the cockpit, the single landing light on the bottom of the ship was still on and in the darkness what you could see of the aircraft brought to mind the Air Force's F-117 stealth fighter only much bigger.

Neil extended his hand "I'm sorry I forgot your name."

"Ted, Ted Sorensen," "O.K. Ted, I'd douse all but a couple of low lights and if you have a tug we can hook to the forward gear and pull her straight in."

"O.K. the hanger windows are all blacked out and there are a couple of low lights in the hanger and the tug is ready, all we have to do is open the hanger doors and pull her in.," said Ted as he started back to the hanger doors .

The eastern sky was showing faint light when Ted and Neil closed the hanger doors with Neil's ship secure inside. Neil climbed back on board shut all system down except the radio, he did not expect to hear from the headquarters until tomorrow.

Ted placed his guards on the outside of the hanger and with nothing more to do Neil took a nap in the ship as he waited for Bonnie.

Neil woke around noon and checked for any radio messages then climbed down out of the ship, he still wore his flight suit. Raymond had just arrived, he was walking around wide eyed as he inspected the outside of the ship, he saw Neil drop down out of a hatch, Raymond walked over with his hand extended. "Wow, I have been skeptical since I first heard this story and now even as I stand here looking at this ship, it still seems unbelievable said Raymond, as he shook Neil's hand, and then reached up and and touched the outside skin of the ship.

"I think I can understand," said Neil, "It's all pretty fantastic and so sudden."

The two men turned towards the small door to the hanger, it just opened and Bonnie walked in, she saw the two men and walked towards them smiling. Neil took several steps towards her grinning.

"How was the trip? everything O.K.," ask Neil.

"Yes, yes fine," answered Bonnie, then her eyes went to the ship.

Raymond walked over acknowledge Bonnie then turned and joined their gaze at the ship.

"What does it run on?" Ask Raymond.

"Electricity, basically," said Neil, "It's complicated, it runs on batteries that are recharged with nuclear fuel, it's not designed to go great distances."

"Wow," said Raymond, "I keep using that word but it's all so fantastic."

Raymond glanced at his watch, "well I've got to go, he looked at Bonnie and Neil, "see my secretary, I'm putting you two on salary now and there will probably be a bonus later, you can stay at the hotel for now and Bonnie go up to advertising, I'll tell my man you will be coming," with that said he turned for the door, before stepping thru the door he turned and gazed at the ship once more then waved and disappeared.

Neil stood in his flight suit and grinned at Bonnie, "I've got to change into jeans."

"They are in the car, I'll get them," said Bonnie as she turned for the door.

Bonnie returned with the jeans, Neil peeled out of the flight suit, checked again to make sure all systems were down except the message center then he took his small communicating instrument and closed the hatch, they went back to the hotel and checked in again, making arrangements for a longer stay.

Neil going to the engineering department dressed in jeans, Bonnie dressed for the business day remained as she was, they were on the sidewalk and ahead of them a couple walked or rather waddled down the sidewalk.

"Will you look at that," said Neil, the couple were past fat they were both obese.

"Remind me the next time I contact the headquarters ship to ask for a diabetes cure and we have got to do something about the worship of food on this planet, said Neil.

"Yes," said Bonnie, "Those two poor people need far more help then they imagine."

They had the elevator to themselves as they rode up to engineering, Neil looked at Bonnie, "We are going to have to design some new lithium batteries as we design the banks of batteries for the electric motor, it should not pose much of a problem."

Bonnie nodded she understood.

"I don't know what Raymond told engineering about the new electric motor, but just treat it as a new idea that engineering came up with and they want to keep it quiet until they are ready to give the story to the media." said Neil.

The bell on the elevator pinged, they were at engineering, the door opened and Neil looked at Bonnie, "meet me for lunch," Bonnie nodded and Neil stepped off the elevator.

Bonnie rode up to advertising and introduced herself to the director, they sat in his office until lunch time.

They discussed all the ramifications of introducing a new product to the market, especially such a revolutionary one and at the same time they had to keep it secret until they were ready.

They discussed hiring a New York advertising firm to help with the event. Bonnie discussed what she knew of the new motor without mention of Neil, finally Bonnie glanced at her wrist it was just past noon she mentioned she had a luncheon appointment, the director nodded he understood and Bonnie got on the elevator for engineering.

Bonnie stopped at the door to engineering and saw Neil, he was moving about from table to table and computer screen to computer screen, his shirt sleeves were rolled up to his elbows and he had a pencil on his ear, he looked up and saw Bonnie, his face burst out in a grin and he started towards her rolling down his sleeves and leaving the pencil on a drawing table.

"Hello love, you ready for lunch," said Bonnie.

"Yes, that sounds good," said Neil, as they stepped into the hallway, Neil said, "they are really enthusiastic," he nodded back towards the engineering department, "they will be ready for production sooner then I expected."

"Where would you like to go for lunch?" ask Bonnie.

"The cafeteria will be fine," said Neil.

As the elevator door opened, Bonnie said, "we have got to go up and see the boss's secretary, I know what she will say, she will want birth dates and social security number etc, I'll give her mine and you make up a birth date and tell her you will have to get back to her on the social security."

"Do you think that will work?" said Neil.

"Yes tell her you were born in 1952 and you will call her back on the social security number, by the time it is processed, we will be into something else so it wont make any difference."

"O.k. you are the boss, said Neil, he absentmindedly pulled the instrument from his ship out of his jean pocket and glanced at it, "everything on the ship is fine, I expect to get an answer from the mother ship anytime now."

The elevator pinged and they stepped off on the floor of executives offices and walked to Raymond's office.

Bonnie made the introductions and the secretary was expecting them.

Everything went according to plan and Bonnie and Neil proceeded to the executive dinning room.

They picked a table for two in a quite corner, they could either get in the cafeteria line or have a waiter serve them, they chose the waiter and he quickly had ice tea on the table and stood back as they studied the menu, made their choice and then sipped the tea.

"How does the public relations job look, you met the head of advertising?" Neil ask.

"Yes, he seems like an O.K. guy, he wants to get all three of the big television networks together when we announce and the big question now is should we get an outside advertising agency, maybe one from New York, to help us," said Bonnie.

"Sounds good, you haven't told him anything about me have you?"

"No, no, he just thinks engineering has come up with a new electric motor that will revolutionize the trucking business," said bonnie.

The waiter began to bring bread and salad.

"Good, that's good," said Neil.

The waiter left.

"Where is Raymond do you know?" Ask Neil.

"No, I think he may have gone out of town," said Bonnie. "I hope he does not say anything about you." Bonnie concluded.

"Oh no, I don't think he will, he knows how vital it is we keep the secret until we are ready," said Neil.

They both began to take the bread and salad.

Neil leaned back, "you know one of the things you don't think about in space travel until you are ready is food, how do you preserve food for five years and sill have it edible and five years of space travel, intergalactic travel is nothing."

They continued to finish lunch and Neil suddenly stopped, used his napkin then reached in his pocket and took out the instrument from his ship, he sat looking at it for a moment then spoke, "speaking of the Mother ship, a message is coming in now, I have to go out to the airport can you come?"

"I think so, the ad director is getting organized, I think he is going to talk to New York, I'll call and tell him where I am going," said Bonnie, "I'll get the check, are you ready?"

Neil paused long enough to tell the waiter how good the lunch was, they road the elevator to engineering Bonnie stopped at a house phone and called advertising to tell them where she was going and Neil told engineering he would be out for the afternoon.

Bonnie used her I.D. at the parking garage to get a company car, the pick-up was still being repaired and they chose a Mercedes, Bonnie was driving, Neil sat next to her, "The mother ship grows their own food, they don't have fields of grain or animal pens but they grow the food from algae, farming is not where my interest lie and I'm not sure how it's done but they produce a complete and nutritious diet and some of it is quite good, they also have a machine shop complete with a forge, actually the mother ship is a small and independent world that picks up raw material and natural recourses as it needs them, the whole thing runs on electricity that is produced by nuclear fusion that charges the batteries."

The mercedes arrived at the airport and Bonnie parked next to the hanger that contained Neil's ship, they got out of the car as a guard approached them, Bonnie showed her I.D. and introduced Neil. Bonnie, Neil and Raymond were the only people permitted in the hanger.

Bonnie and Neil entered the small door next to the big hanger door, Neil pulled out the instrument and studied it for a moment as they walked towards the ship, he pressed a button and a hatch opened on the bottom of the ship, a small ladder extended down. Neil walked towards the ladder indicating Bonnie should follow.

Neil bent down, walked to the ladder and climbed up, Bonnie followed and when her head emerged inside ship, she was looking at the cockpit. There was a single seat for the pilot and instruments were arranged in a semicircle from the pilots left to his right, the glass instruments could be used mentally and as a backup the pilot could lean forward and touch any screen or part of a screen he wanted, the pilots seat had a control stick on the right arm and the throttle on the left. The pilot could control the entire ship mentally if he was incapacitated or in a rest mode he could control the ship by feel.

Neil climbed into the cockpit seat, turned and motioned Bonnie to come on in, behind and to the rear of the pilot there was a small bunk. There was a single green light on the right side of the panel, Neil sat looking at the green light, it flickered several times and a speaker began to chatter, Bonnie could not understand a word of it and after a minute a tape began to unroll from the bottom of the speaker to verify what was said. Neil tore the tape and sat studying it, he slowly folded the tape and put it in his pocket, the tape contained signs and symbols only Neil could interpret, he turned to Bonnie

"Well what do you think?" ask Neil.

"It's fantastic, amazing.., it must be very complicated," said Bonnie as she looked around.

"No actually it's designed for simplicity," said Neil, "with a one pilot it's mostly automatic..."

"Well I guess we need to get back to the office," said Neil.

Bonnie turned for the hatch and climbed down, Neil followed and reached back and shoved the ladder back into the ship as his feet hit the ground, he locked the hatch and turned to Bonnie, they walked out of the small door next to the main hanger door.

As they stepped into the bright sun, they watched a Hawker Beechcraft business jet come to a halt and park on the apron, the lights went out, a door opened and a staircase folded down to the concrete.

Raymond Crane emerged from the door and stepped to the ground, he looked up and saw Bonnie and Neil, he waved and started towards them, he looked at the ground as he walked, he looked up and shook his head then extended his hand to Bonnie and then to Neil.

"You were right," said Raymond, "I've been criss crossing the state talking to associates and people I know who would be interested in investing in a high speed rail system, all I said was I have a radical new electric motor that would make rail travel a lot more appealing and somehow word got to the oil interest and they are all up in arms," there was a pause, "these oil people are piling money into mountains of cash and now they are fracking the earth to get the natural gas out, burning natural gas is good because there is no carbon monoxide, but the fracking is poisoning the ground water, I don't know what these people will do with all their money, where they will live after they make the earth uninhabitable, but there is no reasoning with them," Raymond continued.., "say have 'you got transportation? I need to get back to the office, I dread to think about what's on that computer of mine."

"Yes I have a company car," said Bonnie as she turned and led them around the building to where she was parked.

"I got a message from the headquarters ship confirming the message I sent, and also I sent a request for a cure for diabetes and related circulatory system problems, we have got to do something about the weight and obesity problems on the planet," Neil explained.

"Yes that would be a good thing," explained Raymond.

They arrived at the car, Bonnie drove, Neil sat next to her and Raymond sat in the back. there was no more conversation until Bonnie drove off the airport.

They were on the street driving to downtown Houston, Neil half turned in his seat to address Raymond.

"When I got the answer confirming my original message, it ended in a word that translate in english as 'Stand By', when I have gotten that message in the past, it always meant something was up, it was usually followed by move or return to the headquarters ship or something, it may mean nothing or it may mean I have to move."

Raymond grunted, "Well that's interesting, how are we coming on the drawings for the motor?"

"Drawings for most of the parts are complete and the machine shop should be able to get started forging them and I would say in a week we should have a prototype we can start testing and I have done a drawing redesigning the lithium batteries, the two banks of batteries should last longer and give more power." Neil explained.

"Good, that's good," Raymond answered, "Bonnie what about the P.R., job, how is that coming along?"

"I was with Richard Wilson all morning, we were mapping out an advertising strategy, he is talking to New York this afternoon, he's feeling out the idea of hiring an outside agency to help us.., the only thing I told Richard was we have designed a radical new electric motor," Bonnie answered while keeping her eyes on the road.

"O.K., well that's some good news or at least not more bad," answered Raymond, they then settled down for the ride into town.

After covering some miles and nearing the parking garage, Neil half turned in his seat again and said, "the hi-speed rail is a good idea, it will cut down on fossil fuel burning and keep some carbon out of the air and it will provide fast and efficient transportation, the motor we are designing can be designed up to power a train and the same with the banks of batteries, but that does not do anything for the pollution and the speed is limited."

With this said, Neil made eye contact with Raymond, "being interested in Hi-Speed rail, you are aware of Mag-Lev trains?"

"Yes.., yes, Magnetic Levitation.., I've looked into that and it's just too expensive, you have to build that track very precisely and a good part of it has to be elevated and then there is the right of way problems, and it has to be protected from the wind, it's just too expensive." comments Raymond.

"Yes it's expensive," agrees Neil, "but look at what you get, you will be able to transport an adult across the state for about ten dollars, there is very little if any pollution, the maintenance is minimum and the speed is almost unlimited.., and if you build on existing rail right of ways, you can hold the cost down."

"Yes, well it's something to think about," said Raymond.

They arrived at the parking garage and stopped speaking, from the back seat Raymond suddenly said, "Bonnie you are getting all this ..,?" Bonnie slowed for the entrance to the garage, "Yes, yes, I think so, she answered."

They parked the Mercedes and the three of them were walking down the sidewalk to the entrance to Crane Industries, "like the truck engine you will have to stop the locomotive every 700 to 1000 miles for a slow charge on the batteries but by switching engines, an express train should be able to cross the country in four to six hours." comments Neil.

The three of them entered Crane Industries and stepped on the elevator, "you two keep working, this sounds like some of the plans I have for Hi-Speed Rail, meanwhile I am going up and face my computer," Raymond said.

Neil got off the elevator at engineering, Bonnie rode up to advertising and Raymond continued to the top floor. Entering the advertising offices Bonnie saw Richard Wilson in the outer office, she greeted him with a big smile and ask if he had talked to New York?" "Yes, I talked to two ad agencies and one in particular was really interested and gave a few ideas," answered Richard.

"That's good, I ran into Mr. Crane and he asked how things were going, I told him we had worked out a plan and you were going to talk to New York this afternoon and he was pleased with that."

"How did you see Mr. Crane?" ask Richard.

"I had to drive out to the airport and I met him there, I drove him back to the office," answered Bonnie.

Richard stood nodding his head in the affirmative, yes he understood, he had been to busy to think about it before now but now he understood, before he had been the only conduit for company promotion and advertising information to Raymond Crane and now he had a rival, the woman who called herself head of Public Relations was getting between him and the head office.

Bonnie had not been assigned an office yet and she followed Richard Wilson back to his office, they discussed the plans for revealing the radical new motor to the public, to the media, and Bonnie ask what hiring an outside advertising agency meant.

It was near the end of the business day, the conversation came to a pause.

Richard glanced at his watch, "normally I wait around for that rush hour traffic to settle down before I leave for the day, but I have got to take care of something, I think I'll call it a day," he looked at Bonnie smiling.

Bonnie took the cue and got to her feet, "yes it's been a long day, we can get together in the morning."

Richard said, "yes."

Bonnie turned and walked out of the office.

Richard wanted time alone to think through this latest development.

Bonnie rode the elevator down to engineering, she entered the office and spotted Neil across the room and started towards him smiling, Neil sensed her presence and looked up. He started towards her grinning at her smile.

"They decided to break off a little early in advertising, I'm just floating around until they assign me an office.," said Bonnie.

"Yeah me too," said Neil, "everything is running smooth here, so maybe we could see about some dinner."

Bonnie looked about the room smiling at people on drawing boards and sitting at computer screens, they all accepted Neil enthusiastically as the new boss and they were interested in his de facto woman.

Neil turned smiled, waved good by, took Bonnie's arm and escorted her to the elevator. "What are you in the mood for?" "Should we change into a shirt and tie and find an expensive restaurant?"

"No, let's go as we are, take the pick-up and maybe find some sea food, said Bonnie.

"Seafood?" ask Neil.

"Yes fish," said Bonnie.

"Oh, O.K., the pick-up it is then," said Neil.

Bonnie told the parking attendant they would be taking the pick-up and she asked if he could recommend a good sea food restaurant, "Yes, go over by the ship channel, there are several, Bill's has a good cook," the attendant said.

They sat in a booth at Bill's and Neil has his first fried shrimp with tartar sauce, hush puppies and french fries. "That was good," comments Neil on their way back to the pick-up.

Bonnie drove through the night lights of Houston on their way back to the hotel, Neil did not have the lap top and he sat back in the seat taking in all the sights.

A week later the machine shop at manufacturing had a working model of the electric motor, they had a big freight line tractor, it had a two bunk cab behind the driver's seat and Neil designed an attachment so the clutch and transmission would take the electric motor. They removed the big diesel engine and put the electric motor and two banks of batteries in it's place, after some adjusting everything fit and they closed the hood. Two engineers from engineering climbed into the cab and made a slow circuit of the parking lot and stopped again where they started, the engineers and others opened the hood and inspected everything, it all checked out and they backed up to a trailer and attached it to the tractor, the trailer had sandbags in it to simulate a full load and the driver repeated the circuit around the parking lot and pulled to a stop in the same place, everything worked fine.

The next morning at ten the two same engineers climbed into the cab and with waves and cheers from a small group of employees drove through the chain link fence onto the highway and turned north, on I-10 they curved east and started for the east coast and Jacksonville. They had cell phones and they stayed in constant contact with the company.

They had no diesel noise, no diesel exhaust trailed them, no engine vibration, just the steady hum of the electric motor and the hum and noise of the tires on the road. The engineers watched the voltage meter and as the voltage declined to a certain point they would switch over to the fresh battery, later they would design this to be automatic. They parked at a truck stop in Jacksonville, found an electric outlet, plugged the batteries in and they did not leave the truck except to go to the diner at the truck stop, they slept in the cab.

They had a quick breakfast the next morning and with the sun breaking the sky and sea horizon, they were on the road, heading west out of Jacksonville. It was a repeat of the day before, everything worked fine, they stayed in contact with Houston via cell phone. They turned south off I-10 and drove down to Houston, it was late in the day and as they pulled into the chain link fence at Crane Industries, the company employees were a welcoming committee with welcoming cheers and applause, Raymond was there with Bonnie and Neil, all smiles and grins.

The two engineers climbed down out of the cab, opened the hood and stood peering in.

'How did it go?" said Raymond to the engineer who was driving?

"Fine, wonderful, just great, I would lay money right now we could go on to El Paso without a stop."

"Well we wont do that, you two get some rest, we'll take care of the truck here and you two be ready for an early start for San Diego in the morning."

Raymond answered.

The great news was kept close, confined to Raymond, Bonnie, Neil and the engineering department. The batteries got a slow overnight charge and the same two engineers were in the cab rolling northwest on I-10 as the sky to the east began to show light. The two engineers stayed in touch with Houston by cell telephone everything was becoming routine now as they stayed with I-10 and continued west. The two engineers brought food and water and the only stops were at rest stops and again one stayed with the truck at all times and they switched drivers regularly. They monitored the voltage meter and when the needle dropped to the last line they switched to the fresh battery and the needle jumped to full again.

They picked a truck stop in Arizona, plugged the batteries in and spent the night. The next morning they were moving again at first light, they monitored the voltage, watched their speed and drove on into San Diego. They plugged in the batteries, checked the motor and the transmission fluid, they checked the tires, they crossed the continent and now everything had worked flawlessly.

The next morning with the sky showing color to the east, they were on the road, everything has become routine; they drive into eastern New Mexico, pick a truck stop and plug in; they check in with Houston on a regular basis.

The next morning they are on I-10 again all batteries are freshly charged.., next stop Houston.

The two engineers stayed on the cell phone with Crane Industries and the company knew where they were and exactly when they would arrive. The big freight liner pulled onto Crane Industries property and there at the chain link fence was Bonnie's media event.

They stood crowded around the gate, there were television crews from all the networks in the states as well as crews from Asia and Europe. All the Crane Industries people were there and they slowly parted as the big Freight Liner slowly eased it's way through the gate onto Crane property.

The engineers shut down the big truck pulled the hood latch, got out on each side and walked to the front of the truck. The engineer driver had an NBC mike and camera in his face, "How was it?" "What did you do exactly?" The driver engineer looked at the camera and said, "We just traversed this country from east to west and west to east, from the Atlantic, to the Pacific and back again and we did not burn one drop of fossil fuel..," he stepped around to the front of the truck, opened the hood and said,

"and that's the baby that did it." every camera that could reach it peered into the engine compartment with the small electric engine that was attached to the transmission, it was tiny compared to the big diesel that normally occupied the compartment.

The second engineer driver had a camera and mike thrust into his face, "how much fuel did you burn?" The engineer looked at the reporter, "the only fuel that was burned was by the power company that produced the small amount of electrical power we used to recharge the batteries."

Raymond Crane managed to work his way through the crowd to the front of the truck, he was grinning ear to ear, a mike was thrust into his face, How did you make the engine?" Raymond looked at the reporter, "as you know Crane Industries makes electric motors and this prototype has been in the works for months, years even, we worked with the lithium batteries and suddenly, just recently we had a break through and everything came together..., "still grinning he added, "and this should have some effect on fuel prices."

Bonnie and Neil stood together by the edge of the crowd, they smiled and watched.

After all the questions and answers were exhausted, the crowd began to disperse, the reporters rushing to get their stories ready for the six o'clock news. After the event their was a VIP reception and Bonnie and Neil were there, Bonnie representing public relations and Neil stood just to the side, no mention was made of him or what he was doing there.

The reception was held at Crane Industries main office, someone came in and turned the television on for the 6 O'clock news and they all stood about watching themselves a few hours ago, the 6 O'Clock news carried the story around the world and there were many long faces in the oil and petroleum industries.

Raymond Crane was in conversation with a couple of executives from outside Crane Industries, He glanced over and saw Neil and manage to part from the executives and move over where Neil stood, "Well nothing quite equals success, or having a winner," said Raymond into Neil's ear. Neil turned to him with a big grin, "well that's right.., everybody seems to be accepting the motor."

"Well not everybody, I dread to go back to that computer of mine and find out what the oil and petroleum industries are thinking, and speaking of that, I wanted to talk to you, I came across a man on the computer, I met him before and I didn't have a lot faith that he would be interested, because he owns a railroad on the east coast of Florida and it is primarily freight but to my surprise he is very interested in high-speed rail, a high-speed rail that would be for transporting passengers."

"Well that is a surprise, do you think he will be interested in investing in Mag-Lev, said Neil.

"Yes but he is reluctant, because like me, he is afraid of the cost, he's looked into Magnetic Levitation and he would really like to build one on the east coast of Florida but the cost just stops him," said Raymond.

"Well if he has a rail line on the east coast of Florida, he has the right of way and that is a major part of the cost." Neil explained.

"Yes I know," said Raymond, "the problem now is when he sees this new, motor he will want to design it up to run his freight engines, and that is where any extra cash he has will go.

"That's a possibility alright, and it won't do a thing about the pollution.., well it will cut down a little but the facts are we have got to do something about the number of automobiles burning fossil fuels on the streets and highways." Neil explained.

"Oops, there are two executives from another corporation coming this way, we have got to break this off," said Raymond.

Neil looked up, "all right we can talk about this later, he spotted Bonnie across the room, turned and started towards her.

"Hello Miss Bonnie, Neil said as he approached her grinning.

Bonnie and Neil manage to slip out after the main 6 O'Clock news.

"Well I guess that was successful," said Neil.

"Yes, I believe you are right, so how about dinner, do you want to celebrate?" said Bonnie.

"No, I feel like I have celebrated enough, I would like to just have a quiet dinner and go back to the hotel room and celebrate.," he said grinning at her."

"Mmm that sounds like a good plan," said Bonnie, grinning back.

They had a pleasant dinner in a recommended restaurant and returned to the Hotel.

Bonnie entered the room put her keys down and turned, they embraced, pressing their bodies together, they kissed and began to remove their clothes, forty-five minutes later they were both asleep on the rumpled bed.

Neil put the instrument from his ship on the night table, near midnight it began to ring and vibrate, every light on the instrument was flashing.

Neil sat up and reached for the instrument, he pushed a button and all the lights went out but one, he pushed another button and script and numbers began to run across the small screen, Neil was the only one on earth that could begin to decipher what the message meant, he pushed another button and the instrument went dark except for a green light.

Neil turned to Bonnie who was up on her elbow, "Headquarters is calling I've got to get back to the ship." Neil stood and walked into the bathroom, he quickly shaved and brushed his teeth and came out of the bathroom looking for his bluejeans.

Bonnie had dressed and she went into the bathroom when Neil came out, Bonnie finished dressing and they were both walking out the door within 15 minutes.

"I don't know what it means, I'll have to get to the ship to find out, they sent the message almost as soon as they got mine so it's important," said Neil.

They quickly walked down to the parking garage, an attendant new to Bonnie was on duty, Bonnie showed her I.D. and the attendant was impressed, Bonnie said she wanted a Mercedes the attendant nodded his head yes.

Bonnie and Neil were quickly in a Mercedes on their way to the airport. Between moments of deep concentration Neil would look at Bonnie and speak, "tell Raymond all he needs to do is just scale the electric motor and batteries up to make the high-speed rail system, tell him to put wind turbines on the top edge of each car..," he trailed off and began to concentrate again. Bonnie pulled onto the apron next to the hanger and parked, Neil looked up, "he knows all that, he also knows Mag-Lev is the real answer for high-speed rail, this planet has got to do something about too many automobiles polluting the atmosphere and clogging the streets and highways..," they both got out and showed their I.D.'s to the guard, he opened the small door next to the hanger door, let them in and then got on his phone and called Ted.

Neil opened the hatch at the bottom of the ship and motioned Bonnie to follow him as he climbed up into the ship. He sat in the cockpit and Bonnie sat on the edge of the bunk behind him.

Neil pushed several buttons and a screen to his right lit up and more script and numbers appeared, he sat studying the screen. After a few minutes he turned to Bonnie, "I've got to return to Headquarters, have you got a pen and paper?" Bonnie began to search her purse and handed him a pen and a small note pad.

Neil stopped the screen from rolling and began to write, after several minutes he touched a button and the screen went blank, he turned and handed Bonnie the pen and pad. "that is the cure for diabetes and circulatory system problems, I am not sure I have interpreted it correctly, give it to John Hopkins and Mayo and they will probably figure it out, if not I'll take the time later."

He turned back to the instruments and began to push buttons and pull levers. Suddenly he stopped, stood and walked to the back of the ship, he turned and motioned for Bonnie to follow him as he climbed down the hatch, they stooped and walked out from under the ship, the light was on under the bottom of the ship and as Neil stood and looked up he saw Ted by the small door come walking towards him, Neil extended his hand, "Ted I Have got to take off, attach the tug and we will want to pull her out and point her to the southeast." Ted got busy with the tug and getting the huge doors open.

Neil pulled Bonnie to the side, they kissed and press their bodies together, "I don't know what this means until I get back to headquarters, you need to try and convince Raymond he needs to build the high-speed train but he needs to use Mag-Lev, he needs to cut back on pollution and he needs to get some of these polluting automobiles off the roads and highways, then you need to take Raymond to NASA here in Houston and convince him who I am, tell him the Air Force is working on A.E.S.A. Radar and Li dar and it is the answer for a shield for operating in outer space, it is not guaranteed to stop all high speed missiles but it will deflect most of them, and the more they work on it the better it will get, the only drawback is it takes a lot of power and energy when it is full on, tell the head of NASA I will be in contact and he needs to believe me when I am, take Raymond with you and let him help you convince him."

Neil looked up and saw Ted and the guard were opening the big hanger doors, Ted has already tried to contact Raymond, he left a message and now all he could do was follow the orders of this man who put the ship here in the first place, he had the tug attached and they were ready to pull the tug out on the apron.

Neil pulled Bonnie tighter and kissed her, "I love you Miss Bonnie, he whispered in her ear.

"I love you too," Bonnie whispered back.

"I have the cell phone and as soon as I am close enough, I'll try to call you," said Neil, he kissed her again and released his grip, he stepped over to Ted at the tug, "I'll take off to the southeast using the apron and part of the taxiway, I can tell if I am all clear to the southeast, just keep everybody and everything off the apron," he shook Ted's hand, turned and climbed into the ship, retracted the ladder and locked the hatch. Ted could see only the mass of the ship, the cockpit windows were just a continuation of the ship and Ted began to back the tug pushing the ship out onto the apron.

Neil found the radio frequency for the tower and he told them he was taking off to the southeast. The moon was out but all the tower could see was the low light of the hanger door and the landing lights of what they thought was a large helicopter. Neil sat watching Ted move the ship down pointed to the southeast, he disengage the tug and moved up close to the hanger door. Neil sat thinking for a moment going over the procedures and check list, he reached over and fired the two engines, after he landed he reversed the engines so the thrust would go to the rear of the ship, he stood on the brakes, he was going to take off parallel to the runway to save fuel using part of the taxi way, he released the brakes and the ship was moving, he could feel the thrust as it pushed him back in his seat the ship picked up speed and then he was immobile as the wheels left the tarmac, everything was automatic, the wheels came up into the ship and the doors closed. The control tower would have been puzzled by the two engines on the back of what they thought was a helicopter and if they watched the radar they would have been even more puzzled, the ship was already almost three times the speed of sound and gaining more speed every second as it disappeared to the control tower. Neil was completely immobilized and would remain so until the ship passed through the earths atmosphere and entered low earth orbit. The ship was programed for a direct trip to Mars. When the ship got to Mars it would ricochet off Mars atmosphere and gravity, this would give the ship the sling shot effect slinging it off into outer space still gaining speed every second.

Bonnie stood at the hanger door her eyes still fixed on the last spot in the southeastern sky where Neil disappeared, she turned to Ted, "I'll explain to Mr. Crane in a few hours," it was just past 03:00 A.M. with the blast of the engines thrust gone now, the apron and hanger had the quiet of early morning just before first light, Bonnie turned and walked to the Mercedes and drove back to the hotel, she stood just inside the hotel room door, looking at the rumpled bed. It had all happened so fast, so frantic, she had to take a moment in the stillness of the room to believe it all happened, she reached into her purse and took out the remedy for diabetes that Neil had given her, it looked like it was written in Latin, it looked like a Doctor's prescription, she could not make heads or tails of it. she decided to get back into bed and get a few hours sleep and then go and find Raymond Crane.

Bonnie woke glanced at the clock and saw she would be a little late for the normal work day, she took a quick shower and dressed, she left the hotel heading for Raymond's office, she skipped breakfast and got on the elevator, She got off the elevator and headed for Raymond's secretary's desk, "Is he in?" She ask the secretary.

"Yes he is and He's looking for you," said the secretary, as she nodded towards Raymond's door, "knock first." She said.

Bonnie stepped over to Raymond's door and tapped, she paused a moment and opened the door.

"So there you are," said Raymond as he looked up from his computer.

"Yes I assume you have heard the the news?"

"Well I got a call from Ted that Neil took off," said Raymond.

"Yes," said Bonnie, "his Mother ship was parked just outside our solar system on the edge of deep space, they sent him a message, they had to leave and they would contact him later, he waited and waited and when he finally heard from them they wanted him to return to headquarters for a conference, he assured me he would be back, he just wasn't sure when."

Raymond sat quietly taking this all in, he still did not know which question he should ask, finally he said, "Bonnie you knew him better then anyone and you are the one who misses him the most and it seems to me all we can do is wait."

"Yes, I think that is true," said Bonnie. "He also wanted me to tell you to build the high-speed rail, we need to get some of the polluting automobiles off the streets and highways, he said you knew this and you need to use Mag-lev to build the the high-speed rail, he also said we need to go to NASA and convince the head of NASA who Neil is so when Neil calls him he will listen. Neil said the Air force is working on radar and Li dar and it is the answer for a shield for operating in outer space, he said it would not deflect all missiles but it would stop most of them and the more we work on it the better it will become, the only problem is it takes a lot of power and energy and they are working on that problem now."

"Alright," said Raymond, "and meanwhile we have a high speed rail system to build and I'm getting some very good reports from the media and other places on what a good job you did on your media event."

"Thank you, it's always good to hear good things said about your work."

"Bonny I have been thinking if we build a high-speed rail system on the east coast of Florida and you continue to make presentations, we are going to need an office on the east coast, I think Jacksonville would be the place for that office.., The north south terminus would be there and if we continue on across the country, the east west terminus would be there, what do you say about setting up an office in Jacksonville."

"That's interesting," said Bonnie, "Neil and I discussed the fact that there would be a lot of media events and presentations to sell the high-speed rail and he was for my taking flying lessons rather then getting an automobile and joining in the mass of road and highway traffic."

"Alright now there is another good idea," said Raymond, "and here is a coincidence for you, this landed on my desk yesterday, this young woman has just qualified in Beechcraft aircraft and she is looking for a job.., she has decided on corporate flying rather then airlines, why don't you give her a call, she's probably still here in town." Raymond paused for a moment looking at Bonnie's eyes.., "You haven't had breakfast have you?"

"No, I was up most of the night and I over slept, I came directly here."

"Here take this file, go upstairs have breakfast, read this file and give her a call and see how it goes," Raymond said, handing over the file.

"Alright, I can interview her in the hotel conference room," said Bonnie.

"Good plan, and if she doesn't work out, we can get somebody else, I'm sure there are more to choose from here in Houston," said Raymond.

Cynthia Collins was from Ft. Lauderdale, she was 22 years old, she had just graduated from Embry-Riddle school of aviation at Daytona Beach Florida and she had just finished an indoctrination course in Piper Aircraft including the the Piper PA-46 Mirage and the Hawker-Beechcraft corporate jet, she did not have much flying time, 300 hours, but she had a lot of simulator time and she had a lot of class room time on Beechcraft jet systems, she was single and free to travel and best of all, Bonnie liked her.

Bonnie called Raymond and told him to hire Cynthia.

"O.K." said Raymond, "an here is something else, we have a Piper PA-350 Mirage sitting in the hanger, it's almost new, I bought it for something else that didn't work out and we need to run that engine, send her over there, have her check it out and if it's O.K., take it over to Jacksonville in the morning, and Bonnie there are a lot of messages and communications at the hotel."

"Alright, I'll call her right now," said Bonnie, "and I will check the mail at the Hotel Cindy stopped what she was doing and went over to the hanger she found an A&E mechanic who work for Crane and they both completely checked the Piper Mirage M350, it was the newest version with all the latest technology and safety equipment.

Satisfied Cindy called Bonnie. Bonnie told Cynthia to bring her luggage and be prepared for a flight to Jacksonville early the next morning and be prepared for a stay in Jacksonville.

They both arrived at the field with luggage and topped off the Mirage's fuel tank, A front just past through heading east and they would have a high pressure day all the way to the east coast.

They landed at Mobile and topped off the fuel tank and Bonnie began to get her first flight lessons from Cynthia.

They left the main runway at Mobile and Cynthia gave the controls to Bonnie, she instructed her on how to bank and turn, how to climb, how to descend how to hold a compass heading, they passed Pensacola and Tallahassee following visual flight rules.

Finally passing the Gulf coast, they continued east for Jacksonville, Cindy called Jacksonville international and ask for permission to land, Jacksonville gave permission and the outer marker, Cindy flew there, turned and lined up for final approach. She looked over at Bonnie, "would you like to try a landing?" She ask.

Bonnie looked over with a grin, "yeah, sure, do you think I can?"

Cindy returned her grin, put the flaps down and said, "take the controls.., now if I say give me the controls, just drop everything and let me have it." "Right O.K." said Bonnie as she adjusted her seating and took the yoke in her hands.

The Piper Mirage M350 is a single engine prop aircraft with tricycle landing gear, it is a dependable easy to fly aircraft.

"Alright," said Cindy, "we are on final approach, the runway is dead ahead, just hold this heading and start your descend, Cindy ease back on the throttle and let the speed come down and watch the heading.., there, there is the runway, you want to put the nose wheel on that line, but you want to put the mains down first, ease the throttle back a little, that's good, you are looking good, your speed is just about right, bring her down with the nose on the center line, let the mains touch first, that's good, you are looking good, keep her level," 'CHIRP', both main wheels touched at the same time. "good, bring the yoke back, throttle back, now, let it slow and hold the center line, that's good, let me have the controls now." Cindy gently put both hands on the yoke and eased the throttle up just a bit as she looked for a turn off the main runway, she saw one up ahead and eased the throttle back a bit and turned onto the taxi way.

Cindy looked over at Bonnie smiling, "that was a good landing, you have what is called a good stick in the flying business."

"Well I hope it wasn't just beginners luck." Said Bonnie

"No you have a feel for it," said Cindy as she looked for the hanger to put the Piper Mirage in.

They secured the Piper and took their luggage, Bonnie went to the car rental while Cindy went up and closed out her flight plan.

They drove into the city and checked into the hotel where Raymond stayed when he was in town, Raymond was right there was a lot of mail.

Bonnie got two rooms, She had Cindy look into finding an employment agency that could send over experienced receptionist she could interview, and then she took over the mail. There were E-mails, snail mail, and just phone calls, she called back to Houston when she needed to ask a question.., Bonnie stayed with the mail most of the afternoon and as she was just finishing, she got a call from Houston, it was Raymond's secretary, "could she have dinner with Raymond tomorrow evening, he will call from the airport.

Bonnie used the next morning interviewing receptionist and finally settled on two, both were experienced but one was actually still working, her company was moving and she could keep her job and move with the company, but she wanted to stay there so she was looking for a job with a new company. Bonnie liked her and preferred her. She put the second application for Raymond to see so he could have a choice.

With the afternoon wearing on Bonnie was back in her room when, her cell phone rang, it was Raymond, he was at the airport.

"Can I pick you up?" Bonnie ask.

"No, I'm leaving now," said Raymond, "I'll meet you at the hotel we can have dinner."

"Can I bring Cindy," Bonnie ask

There was a pause.., "can you trust her?"

"Yes, she is teaching me to fly, and she is helping me with the presentations and she is becoming very enthusiastic about the high-speed rail, I haven't told her about Neil yet but she is very enthusiastic about Crane Industries.

"You are going to need some help so I guess if you trust her you may as well bring her so she knows what is going on.

Raymond's room was two adjoining rooms one was the bed room and the other was used for conferences, Raymond called Bonnie and told her to come up to the room.

Bonnie and Cindy arrived and Raymond got them seated in the conference room and pulled an instrument out, he began to go about the room stopping at the lamps and tables and looking at the interment.

"I am going to assume you know what that was all about," said Raymond as he looked at the two woman, they both nodded.

"I may look a little paranoid but I have found the less that is known about your plans the easier it will be to complete them, now don't get complacent," he added, someone can walk in here in the next twenty minutes and leave a listening device or bug as they are commonly called and it could pick up every sound in the room, they have become very sophisticated."

Raymond looked at Cynthia, "so miss Cynthia I understand you are interested in high-speed rail systems."

"Yes, I've read the history you have so far and I find it very exciting, answered Cindy.

"O.K., that is very good," said Raymond, "now the reason I flew over here today..," he paused again then said, "we need to keep this quite because to repeat, the less known about your plans the better," he looked at the two women who gave a slight nod then he added, "I just got word, some people in the Florida legislature have plans to run a high-speed rail system from Tampa-St. Petersburg over to Orlando, now if that happens they will eventually run a spur down to Miami then run the line up through central Florida, through all that farm land next to I-75, all the way to Atlanta and leave central and northeast Florida high and dry."

"Well that doesn't make much sense," said Bonnie.

"No it does not and that is a good example of the enemy, the enemies you will encounter in a project like this.., well maybe enemy is too harsh a word, maybe opposition would be a better word, I suspect some of the people in the Florida legislature own the land going up i-75 or they know who does and their interest would be in getting the high-speed rail going up central Florida from Orlando and then on to Atlanta and up the east coast to Washington, New York and on to Boston," Raymond paused for a moment then continued, "to buy all that land for right of way would make a few people rich but it would add billions to the cost."

"Well to repeat, that makes no sense," said Bonnie.

"Yes," said Raymond, "and as dumb as it is, it's so true of what we will run into as we come closer to realizing a Florida east coast high-speed rail system."

"Now the reason I flew over here today.., on Friday there is a committee meeting in the Florida legislature, it's open to the public and anyone can come.., Bonnie I'm wondering, you have three days, do you think you and Miss Cynthia here could get a High-Speed Rail System presentation ready by then?"

"I think I can, I have all the material from the media event for the new electric motor," said Bonnie.

"Good, you have the material from the media event," he paused and reached down and took a couple of video's from his bag, "here are a couple of video's from advertising, Richard Wilson sent them over, they are of Mag-Lev trains in Japan, China, and Germany, watch them and see if there isn't something there you can use."

"Magnetic Levitation, said Bonnie, "Neil was insisting I tell you to use Mag-Lev on any high speed train you build.

"Yes, I know his thinking on that and he is probably right, the big problem is cost and with all the other problems we are running into, I'm not sure we can handle Meg-Lev." Raymond explained.

"Yes well we still have the electric motor, and as we try to over come some of these problems of right of way, maybe we can get enough investors that will invest in Mag-Lev," Bonnie said.

"Yes Miss Bonnie, now that's the right kind of thinking we need here," said Raymond, he paused for a moment.., "I have a real estate man working on finding us an office here in Daytona Beach, Bonnie have you found us a receptionist?"

"Yes," said Bonnie, "she paused as she reached down and took files out of her briefcase, here are two, they are both well qualified, this one has been in the business for a while, but I favor this one, she is working now but her company is moving and they want her to go with them but she wants to stay here, she is the right age and as I say, well qualified."

"Alright, I'll look them over," said Raymond as he took the files.., "O.K., are you two ladies ready for dinner?"

He got nods from both Bonnie and Cindy.

"Alright, if you want to go back to your rooms, I'll meet you in the lobby and I thought we would go to the same restaurant we were at last time, it's a short walk, and I need a walk.

Cindy and Bonnie stood in the lobby waiting for Raymond, "That's the first time you met him isn't it?" said Bonnie.

"Yes, he's very impressive," said Cindy.

"Yes and the power and influence he has makes him even more impressive." said Bonnie, "oh here he comes now."

They walked to the restaurant and were quickly seated at Raymond's favorite table, Raymond pulled out his instrument and waved it over the table, the waiter had menus in their hands and everyone began to study.

"I'll have ice tea," said Bonnie, Raymond and Cindy nodded and the waiter left the table.

Their was a moment of silence and Bonnie folded her menu and laid it on the edge of table, "I'm wondering if this isn't a good time to discuss Neil Conrad."

"Bonnie you know him more then anyone else and if Cindy is going to be working on the promotions with you, it would probably be good idea to fill her in on Neil," Raymond explained.

Bonnie looked at Cindy and began to explain, "Neil Conrad is the creator of the new electric motor, but he is a lot more then that. Mr. Crane here and I are the only ones who know this and Cindy I can not be too demanding on this but you can not whisper a word of this until we are ready to release this information..," Bonnie paused in silence for a moment as she collected her thoughts, "Neil is not of this earth he is from another solar system" and then Bonnie started at the service station in the desert where she first met Neil and continued to give the full story. The waiter came with the ice tea and Raymond ask him to give them a few minutes before he took their orders.

Bonnie continue the story until she got to the point where they tested the new electric motor and Cindy put her application in at Crane Industries.

There was a moment of silence and then Raymond got the waiters attention from across the room and motioned him over. The waiter took their orders and left.

They sat in silence for a moment and then Cindy spoke, "that's some story, are you sure he's who he says he is, I mean it's not some kind of hoax."

"Oh no," said Bonnie, "he landed his ship at the field and put it in the hanger, it was at night and nobody saw it but a couple of guards, and they didn't know the full story..."

"Wow, a real alien.., an Extraterrestrial, so their is life in the universe besides planet earth?" said Cindy.

"Yes and wait until you meet him, he's coming back," said Bonnie.

She looked into Raymond's eyes "and speaking of that, Neil insisted that I take you over and talk to the head of NASA and convince him who Neil is because Neil is going to call him and he needs to believe Neil when he does.

"I'm not so sure I can convince him of anything especially that story," said Raymond.

"Neil said to tell him the Air force is working on A.E.S.A. radar and Li dar and it is the answer for a shield for operating in outer space, it is not guaranteed to stop all high speed missiles but it will deflect most of them and the more they work on it the better it will become, the only drawback is it takes a lot of power and energy when it is full on, they are working on that now trying to bring the power it requires down when it's in use." Bonnie explained.

"You mean this radar is a secret, or at least it's not common knowledge," said Raymond.

"Yes, that was the impression I got when he told me about it, we were in such a rush for him to take off..," Bonnie explained.

"Good then maybe we can get NASA'S attention with that." said Raymond.

"I hope so," said Bonnie.

Raymond looked at Cindy, "What is your opinion on this Miss Cindy, do you believe we had an extraterrestrial here and he is coming back?"

"It's a beautiful story, but I believe if I had to bet on it, I would like a little more proof," said Cindy.

"Yes you and just about everybody else," said Raymond as he picks up his knife and fork.

"I'm sure Neil will have plenty of proof when he gets back here," said Bonnie, as she held her salad fork, and speaking of that, Neil was adamant that we use Meg-lev on the high speed train.., he was concerned about the increasing number of vehicles on the streets and highways and the more and more carbon monoxide going in to the atmosphere from burning fossil fuels.

Bonnie put her salad fork on the plate and continued, "I have been studying the Cosmos and our solar system in my spare time since Neil left, and millions of years ago when the solar system was forming, planet Earth and planet Venus were very similar, they are about the same size, and Venus is a little closer to the sun but millions of years ago they both had oxygen and water and for some reason planet Venus began to form volcanos all over the planet and as they erupted they began to fill the atmosphere with carbon monoxide and heat and now you not only can not breath the poisonous carbon monoxide but the heat would boil you alive. Here on planet Earth we are burning and cutting down the forest that gives us oxygen and all the power plants are burning fossil fuels that are putting poisonous carbon monoxide into the atmosphere plus all the vehicles are burning fossil fuels and putting carbon monoxide in the atmosphere. I fear we are going to look up someday not to far in the future and find we don't have enough oxygen to breath and if we continue to over populate this earth, we are going to see mass starvation." Bonnie paused from speaking and suddenly said, "Oh I'm sorry, I didn't mean to bring so much gloom to the dinner table."

"No no, said Raymond, you and Neil are right it's just that no one wants to believe you and they don't want to believe you because they will have to change and nobody wants to change and nobody wants to invest in mag-lev because the profits will be slow in coming.., so Bonnie it's going to be up to you and Cindy here to convince them, convince them they need to invest in the future of this planet."

"You are right about that and you are right about putting the High Speed Rail System here in Daytona Beach, if we bring the High Speed Rail System up the east coast of Florida and then run it across the panhandle to Pensacola and follow I-10 all the way to Los Angles and San Diego.., Atlanta, Montgomery, New Orleans, Houston, all of the cities and states will look at that and they will want it and they will find a way to get it," said Bonnie.

"Yes Bonnie," said Raymond, "and so it's up to you and Cindy here to go over to that Florida legislature and convince them Daytona Beach is the place for the northern and eastern terminus of the High Speed Rail System."

"Hopefully we will be able to find some people interested in investing in Mag-Lev," said Bonnie.

Cindy sat quietly taking this all in, she learned things she did not know or even think about.

The conversation turned to small talk, as everyone picked up their knives and forks and began to eat the dinner.

The conversation came to a halt and Raymond suddenly spoke, "Bonnie if you need anything to make your presentation, call advertising, I'm sure Richard Wilson can get it for you, you two have the right attitude for this project and Neil is right, Magnetic - Levitation is the answer, I'm just not sure we can pull it off." He put his silverware down drained his ice tea and used his napkin. "Ladies I have got some work to do in my room, If you are ready, we can walk back to the hotel and Bonnie if you need anything don't hesitate to call my secretary."

The cooler air off the river was pleasant as they walked back to the hotel, they parted in the hotel lobby, "Bonnie, here is my private number if you need anything or a problem comes up, you can reach me if you need to," said Raymond, as he stepped on the elevator leaving the two ladies in the lobby.

"So O.K.," said Cindy, "what's Mag-Lev or Magnetic-Levitation?"

"Well lets see," said Bonnie, she thought a moment and then said, "do you remember when you were a child did you ever play with magnets?"

"Probably, I don't recall," answered Cindy.

"O.K. well here.., a magnet has two poles, north pole and south pole, if you take one magnet's north pole and move it very close to the second magnet's south pole, just before they touch the second magnet will jump out of the way, now that is essentially what Mag-Lev or Magnetic Levitation is all about, China, Japan, and Germany have Mag-Lev trains, China has one running from the city of Shanghai out to their airport, this is a short distance, and Germany has had an accident with theirs and that is about as much as I know about the recent history but what I can tell you is, it's very expensive to build Mag-Lev, and the reason for this is it has to be very precise, you can not have warped bent or uneven rails or guide ways, and you have to build a covering on the rails so the train is not blown off the tracks by the wind, when the train starts, it is lifted off the rails and suspended in mid air by the magnetism, then the magnetism moves the train down the track and the speed can be almost as fast as the airlines and it is best if the tracks are elevated to keep vandalization and other obstacles out of the way, once it is built there is no pollution, or the only pollution is by the power companies that furnish the electricity, maintenance is very little," Bonnie explained as they sat in the hotel lobby."

"Let's see if there is a T.V. set here that will play these videos Raymond gave us," said Bonnie, they walked towards the hotel desk and they were pointed to the conference room, they walked in and saw a T.V. set, they inserted the videos and sat down. All three videos were very short but they showed what a Mag-Lev train would look like, they were impressive. After the third video ended, Bonnie and Cindy both sat back.

"That certainly is impressive," said Cindy.

"Yes and can you imagine after the cost of building the train, you could transport an adult across the state for about $10.00 and once the track is in you could go from Jacksonville to San Diego in about four or five hours."

Bonnie explained.

"That to is impressive," said Cindy "and once it is up and running, and the inside of the coaches are as nice as the videos show, you can see where a lot of the automobile driving and the carbon monoxide in the atmosphere would come to an end."

"Yes and now we have got to go over to Tallahassee and convince those people not only to build in Jacksonville but to build the Mag-Lev." said Bonnie.

Raymond Crane had a man at the Florida legislature and he made an appointment for the presentation, Bonnie and Cindy would make their presentation right after lunch, until Friday, the two wrote and rewrote the presentation until they were satisfied with it.

Early on Friday morning they took the Piper Mirage and flew over to Tallahassee, during lunch they set up their presentation and when the committee returned from lunch, Bonnie gave the presentation, she started with how the Florida east coast would be left high and dry if the high speed train did not run through Jacksonville. After that she gave a presentation on how the train would work in Florida then she showed the videos and took questions.., after the questions died down, She and Cindy took their gear and left the committee room. They decided it would be better to go to lunch and let the committee hash out all the questions and arguments without them there.

Cindy let Bonnie take off and fly back to Jacksonville, after Bonnie landed the Piper, Cindy took over the controls and taxied back to the hanger, Bonnie could not count the flight time because she had not soloed yet.

They were in the car driving back to the hotel when Bonnie's cell rang,

"Hello?" "Oh hi," it was Raymond.

"You did it again," said Raymond, "I had a man there and he said they were excited and enthusiastic to learn that someone is already working on a high speed rail system and your presentation of Mag-Lev has sold them all, of course they do not know the cost yet.., and here is some more we have an appointment with NASA on Monday morning at 10 am."

"Oh thank you, we left early for lunch thinking it would be better to let the committee answer any questions among themselves," said Bonnie.

"Well it was a good idea because everybody seems ready to put the high speed train in Jacksonville," said Raymond, then he continued.., "Bonnie, Cindy is checked out in the Hawker Beechcraft business Jet and I need a faster and larger aircraft.., why don't you and Cindy fly the Piper Mirage over here in the morning, I am going to trade the Mirage in for a larger jet and you and Cindy can take the Beechcraft, it will be larger, faster and more comfortable.

"Certainly we can do that, how is NASA are they ready to listen to Neil when he calls?"

"I didn't talk to anyone, I thought it best to let my secretary make the appointment and we can try to convince him when we get there." Said Raymond.

"Cindy is a good pilot and she will be happy to hear this news.., we will see you tomorrow." Bonnie said.

"O.K. call me when you get in," said Raymond as he clicked off.

Bonnie clicked her cell off, she looked over at Cindy driving, and smiled, "did you get any of that?"

"Not really," Cindy glanced over at Bonnie then put her eyes back on the road.

"That was Raymond, he had a man at the meeting, and he said we really pulled it off, the committee was enthusiastic and excited that someone was actually working on a high speed train and it was going to Jacksonville, They were in the city traffic now and Bonnie paused from talking as Cindy got busy with the traffic. "Let's wait until we get to the hotel."

O.K. said Cindy without taking her eyes off the street.They parked the automobile and went to their rooms and then met in the lobby, "Do you want to go back to the same restaurant, I could use the walk?" said Bonnie.

"Yes that sounds good," said Cindy, "I need the walk too," they were both dressed in Ladies business suits and wearing business shoes, high heels no spikes.

"We sold them on a high speed train for the east coast?" said Cindy, starting the conversation.

"Yes high speed rail for the east coast, terminating in Jacksonville and eventually running the line across the panhandle to the west coast and Raymond said they were very enthusiastic about Mag-Lev.., but they have not heard the cost of Mag-Lev yet so don't get to excited."

They came to an intersection and the conversation stopped while they waited to cross, they got to the other side and Bonnie continued, "Raymond is very pleased with the presentation we gave and he is going all out to build the high speed rail and he needs a larger and faster corporate jet, he wants us to fly the Mirage over to Houston in the morning and he is going to trade it in on a larger jet and he wants us to take the Beechcraft, you are checked out in the Hawker-Beechcraft corporate jet, and you can handle it, right?"

"Gosh yes," said Cindy, "I haven't seen the Crane Industries Beechcraft yet but normally they have plumbing and a refrigerator and it needs a copilot to fly.

"But they are a lot faster, right?" Comments Bonnie.

"Yes, yes they are and they will climb about as high as you want to go," says Cindy.

The early evening walk back to the hotel was pleasant and they parted in the hotel elevator, "set the alarm for 5 O'clock, we can get breakfast at the airport, but plan on staying in Houston until Tuesday or Wednesday, Bonnie said.

Bonnie drove the auto rental to the airport and checked it in while Cindy filed her flight plan, "the weather is going to be good all the way to Houston," said Cindy, as they met in the restaurant, they had a quick breakfast and went out and checked the Mirage, loaded their luggage, topped off the fuel, climbed aboard and Cindy called the tower for clearance to taxi, they parked at the end of the take off runway and Cindy called the tower for permission to take off, the tower cleared them and Cindy offered the controls to Bonnie, Bonnie looked at Cindy with a big smile and took the controls, she eased the throttle forward and steered out on the runway, she set the front wheel on the center line and began to ease the throttle forward, the Mirage began to pick up speed, gaining and gaining until the Mirage just insisted on leaving the concrete and Bonnie eased the yoke back and they were on their way.

"We will top off the tanks at Biloxi, Mississippi," said Cindy and then she gave Bonnie the compass heading and Bonnie turned for Biloxi on the Gulf.

Cindy watched Bonnie very closely, leaving her with the controls all the way to Biloxi, at Biloxi she got permission to land and then they saw the field and Cindy told Bonnie to line up for final approach.

Landing is the hardest part of flying and Bonnie did this before at Jacksonville and she followed what Cindy said, O.K. good, that's good, ease back on the throttle, let her slow, that center line is what you are after, keep her level, that's good let her slow down, keep her level, that's good.., Chirp, one chirp, both wheels on the concrete at once, another good landing, "very good, If I were qualified I would say you are soloed now," said Cindy, "let me take it now, Cindy took the yoke and began to steer to the main hanger.

Bonnie turned and smiled at Cindy, "we need to do that, get me soloed, how much more complicated is the Beechcraft then this aircraft?"

"It's complicated and it needs two pilots but I am sure we could handle it," answered Cindy, as she parked the Mirage and called for the fuel truck.

Both of them got out of the aircraft and stretched their legs, "why don't you go find the ladies room, I don't like to leave the aircraft when we are just stopped for fuel," said Cindy, "try that door there," she said, indicating a door for the hanger.

The fuel truck arrived and began to fuel the Mirage while Cindy watched.

The fuel truck was almost finished when Bonnie came out of the door and walked towards the the Mirage.

"Can you pay the fuel truck while I go," said Cindy. "Yes through that door and turn to your left," answered Bonnie, "it's clean."

They both got back into the aircraft and Cindy called the control tower for permission to take off, she was given the main runway and she started the engine and began to taxi to the holding area for the runway, at the holding area Cindy put the brakes on, she began to run the engine up and then let it come back to idle while she set the flaps for takeoff then called for permission to take off.

Bonnie sat studying her every move and when control gave permission to take off, Cindy looked at Bonnie and indicated she take the yoke. Bonnie grinned and took the yoke and released the brakes, she moved over on the main runway and put the front wheel on the center line, she looked over at Cindy got a nod and she began to push the throttles forward, The Mirage started moving, gaining speed, Bonnie held the yoke forward the speed building and the Mirage began to shake and vibrate as if screaming let me fly, let me fly, Bonnie glanced at the speed indicator and eased the yoke back, suddenly the screaming stopped, everything smoothed out and the Mirage climbed away leaving the Biloxi concrete behind.

Bonnie flew the Mirage on to Houston, the high pressure day was ending with clouds forming on the western horizon as they approached Houston, Cindy called Houston control for permission to land.

Bonnie was flying with confidence now and she flew to the outer marker and then picked up final approach and made another one chirp landing.

They were not at Houston's main airport, they were at the small field where Crane Industries had a hanger, Cindy took the controls and taxied over to the Crane Industries hanger, She parked the Mirage, set the brakes and shut down the engine. They both looked up and saw Ted come out of the hanger door and walk towards them.

Bonnie left Ted and Cindy to talk and went into the hanger to make a phone call to Raymond to tell him they had arrived.

"Fine, you have arrived," said Raymond on the phone, "do you think Cindy can handle the Beechcraft O.K.?

"Yes I left her and Ted talking, Cindy seemed pleased with the opportunity and I am sure she can handle it."

"Good well you and Cindy take off and make a short familiarization flight as soon as Cindy is ready.., I'm sure Ted can give her anything she needs."

"Now on Monday morning at 10: O'Clock we have an appointment at NASA headquarters, I have never met the head of NASA and as I said I had My secretary make the appointment with his secretary so on Monday morning it is going to be up to us to go over there and convince him that Neil is an extra terrestrial, he speaks fluent english, he came in here on a space ship and he is coming back and he wants NASA to make accommodations for him to land."

"Yes, I think that about covers it," said Bonnie.

"O.K.., you keep all this in that pretty head of yours over the weekend and on Monday morning it's going to be up to you, mostly, to convince NASA who Neil is.., and I must say I was very skeptical right up until I saw the ship in the hanger."

"Yes I know and Neil can be very convincing in person, but on that phone or the radio, I'm not so sure," said Bonnie.

"Well we will find out Monday morning," said Raymond, "meanwhile you and Cindy be careful in that Beechcraft."

"Oh, we will, we will, said Bonnie and she hung up and went to find Cindy.

Cindy had taken all the luggage out of the Mirage and put it in the hanger and Ted was busy getting the Beechcraft ready to pull it out of the hanger.

Bonnie walked over to Cindy, "Raymond was glad we had arrived, he and I have an appointment on Monday morning to try and convince NASA Who Neil is and meanwhile we can take a familiarization flight with the Beechcraft and he said to be careful."

"I always try to do that," said Cindy.

Ted had the Beechcraft on the tug and he was pulling it through the hanger door.

"We can just stay on the ground and become familiar with the Beechcraft and fly tomorrow," said Cindy.

"O.K., is flying copilot on a Beechcraft jet complicated?" ask Bonnie.

"Not really, it's just flying, you need to know how to fly, I mean there is nothing profoundly complicated, if you can fly it's just a matter of getting checked out in that particular type, but jets are more complicated."

"Alright we will do some dry runs here, why don't you help Ted while I call the Hotel and make reservations," said Bonnie.

"Right," said Cindy as she started walking towards Ted on the Tug.

Bonnie walked into the hanger called the hotel and got two rooms and when she came back out Ted was driving the tug back into the hanger and Cindy had the Beechcraft door open, she was about to climb aboard, Bonnie hurried over and they climbed on aboard together.

"My look at that," said Cindy as she put her hand on the small counter top, "we have plumbing and a fridge and sink, she looked up, "and through that door there should be a bathroom or at least a toilet."

The Beechcraft had been custom designed and built for Crane Industries and as Bonnie and Cindy walked through they realized they would have a much more comfortable ride.

"Here let's check out the cockpit," said Cindy as she turned around and started towards the front of the aircraft, "wow look at this, complete glass cockpit, come sit in the copilot seat," said Cindy.

They spent the rest of the day making dry runs, they even used the turned off mikes to communicate with the control tower, using the proper language and protocol, At the end of the business day Bonnie felt she knew enough about the Beechcraft, she could be the copilot with Cindy's guidance.

"We need to get into the air," said Cindy, as she looked over at Bonnie, "What do you say we take a flight down to Corpus Christi in the morning?"

"That sounds good," said Bonnie, "why don't you get the flight plan ready while I go talk to Ted, see if he wants to leave the Beechcraft outside or take it back in, we should leave before daylight, and I need to find us a ride to the hotel.

Ted decided to top off the fuel tanks and then bring the Beechcraft back inside the hanger for the night.

Bonnie found someone driving into the city, she got Cindy and the luggage and they took advantage of the ride.

They each went to their rooms and freshen up for dinner.

"What are you in the mood for?" Bonnie asked when they met in the lobby.

"I don't know.., what do you think," said Cindy.

"I don't know either but if we are going to take off before first light, we need to get a good nights sleep, why not eat here in the hotel?" Bonnie, said "Good, that sounds good to me," said Cindy, "I Know I can use the sleep."

They walked to the hotel restaurant, afterwards they stopped by the desk and made sure they both go a wake up call for the morning.

It was still dark when the wake up calls came, and they both got about 8 hours sleep. the restaurant was not open yet so they walked to the Crane garage and got a car from the attendant and drove to the airport.

They stopped for coffee on the way and the attendant at the airport, an A&E mechanic opened the door for them, Bonnie showed her ID and ask to have the Beechcraft towed out onto the apron, Ted apparently told the mechanic they would be coming and he was completely cooperative.

With the Beechcraft out on the apron, Cindy and Bonnie climbed aboard and began the preliminaries for take off, Cindy in the left seat, she called the tower for permission to taxi to the runway, at the runway she ran the engines up, set the flaps, looked over at Bonnie and called the tower for permission to take off, the tower gave permission and Cindy looked at Bonnie again and began to ease the throttles forward, holding the front wheel on the center line, she opened the throttles all the way and held it until the Beechcraft began to insist on flying and Cindy eased the yoke back and the Beechcraft left the concrete behind, "gear up," said Cindy, without looking at Bonnie, Bonnie pulled the lever to bring the landing gear up, Cindy was preparing the auto pilot for 28,000 feet, the altitude the tower gave them and the altitude they would fly to Corpus Christi.

All of these things they had practiced the day before and they would continue until it all became routine and second nature.

At 28,000 feet the auto pilot stopped climbing and leveled off, Cindy check the flaps and made sure everything was correct for speed at level flight, she looked over at Bonnie and grinned, "what do you think?"

"It's much quieter, and its hard to believe we are at 28,000 feet." Bonnie answered.

"Yes the cabin pressure is at about 8,000 feet and this auto pilot is the latest technology, it really takes over a lot of the work.., but you still have to know how to handle the aircraft in case something goes wrong." Cindy explained, "Would you like to take the auto pilot off and hold it for a while, get the feel for it?" Bonnie nodded her head smiling,

"O.K. take the controls, there isn't much to do, hold it level and make sure you are on course and keep scanning the the glass and make sure everything is O.K.," said Cindy.

Bonnie had the controls and without looking at Cindy, She said, "It's a lot more delicate and sensitive."

"Yes it is but you will get use to that," said Cindy, "I have the auto pilot set for the outer marker at Corpus Christi, when we get there, would you like to turn final and try a landing?"

"Yes, yes I would," said Bonnie without taking her eyes off the instrument panel.

Control tower was pretty quiet, the traffic was light for this part of Texas and it was the ending of a very high pressure day with a change coming from the north west, tomorrow would be clouds for Houston. "Would you like to put the auto pilot back on and we can go over the procedures?"

"Yes alright," said Bonnie as she looked over at Cindy.

Cindy began to push buttons and then looked over at Bonnie indicating she should let go of the yoke, they had each others confidence now and they trusted each other.

With the auto pilot flying the jet again they could discuss what was on their minds, "trying a landing at Corpus Christi would be better," Cindy said, 'The air space at Houston is pretty crowded especially by the time we get back, "Yes, yes, I understand, said Bonnie.

"O.K. the traffic is probably light there, that is light compared to Houston, so we can try it." Cindy said.

While the auto pilot was flying, they went into the procedure for the cockpit.., and finally Cindy checked the glass screen and said, "we are getting close to Corpus Christi, are you ready to fly to the outer marker?" Cindy asked.

"Yes," said Bonnie.

"I was thinking of just making a touch and go, but maybe we should land, top off the fuel tanks and see about some lunch, what do you think?" ask Cindy.

"Yes, that sounds good," answered Bonnie.

"I could use the the potty," said Cindy, "but I think I will wait until we get down and then we wont have to change it."

Bonnie gave her a nod, and Cindy picked up the mike and called Corpus Christi, she identified the aircraft and ask for permission to land.

Corpus Christi gave her the heading for the outer marker and permission to land, "Roger that," said Cindy.

Cindy turned to Bonnie and indicated she take the yoke, then she turned off the automatic pilot, they discussed the landing with the auto pilot on and now Bonnie took the yoke, eased the throttles back, set the flaps for landing and prepared the aircraft for slowing down for the outer marker and she began to lose altitude.

Cindy was watching and encouraging her every move, "that's good, right, that's good."

Bonnie slowed the aircraft and lost the altitude for the landing, she turned at the outer marker for final approach and Cindy lowered the landing gear, Bonnie made a one chirp landing.

"With the weather changing we need to get back to Houston as soon as we can." said Cindy.

They topped off the fuel tanks and found fast food sandwiches on the field, then Cindy took the controls and they were back in the air.

Cindy got her altitude from the control tower, she was assigned 28,000 feet again, She put the aircraft on auto pilot and at 28,000 feet it leveled off and Cindy checked to see all the instruments were functioning together, and she turned to Bonnie, "when we get back to Jacksonville we are going to have to find a qualified pilot to solo you so you can start counting the hours you are flying or else I will have to get qualified..."

"What are you going to do tomorrow morning, just try to convince NASA that we had an alien visitor and he is coming back and he wants to land at Cape Canaveral?"

"Yes essentially that's about it," answered Bonnie.

"That may be a lot harder to do then it seems at first," said Cindy, "I know you are honest and sincere but with nothing but the story it may be very hard to convince NASA that the story is true."

"Yes, I know and I have been thinking about it," said Bonnie.

"How about Mr. Crane does he have anything more convincing?" Cindy ask.

"If he has, he hasn't told me about it, said Bonnie.

"Well do you want me to turn the auto pilot off and let you practice some flying," Cindy ask.

"Yes let's do that, and you can brief me on the glass cockpit some more.

They continued flying and instructing back to Houston, finally Cindy looking at the glass cockpit said, "well we are getting close now so let me take over, with all this traffic and a weather change coming, we may as well get down."

Cindy called the field with Crane's hanger and ask for permission to land, permission was granted and Cindy eased the throttles back and began to get the aircraft ready to land.

Cindy landed with no problems, Bonnie was watching and learning. Cindy taxied over to the Crane hanger and parked the Beechcraft. Bonnie got out of her seat and said, "I'll go call in and tell them we have arrived," She looked up, "here comes Ted, you can talk to him," she climbed down out of the jet and started towards the hanger, she passed Ted, smiled and said, it was a good trip, everything worked fine.

"Good, that's always good," said Ted as he continued on to the Beechcraft.

Bonnie called Raymond's secretary, "he's out," said the secretary. "O.K., just tell him we are back and Cindy and I will go over the Tallahassee presentation and see what we can improve and I'll see him monday morning and we can go over what we are going to say at NASA."

"O.K., I Will see he gets the message," said the secretary.

Bonnie walked back out to the Beechcraft and listened to the conversation between Cindy and Ted about maintaining the Beechcraft.

"Yes, Bill Evans is the man's name and he is a top A&E mechanic, and engineer and he knows the Hawker-Beechcraft jet, I don't know if he is open for employment, but check with him and if he is not maybe he can recommend somebody else.

"O.K." said Cindy as she looks up at Bonnie's approach, "Ted here is recommending an A&E mechanic over at Jacksonville we can use," Cindy said to Bonnie,

"That's good we will need one," said Bonnie, "where is he in Jacksonville She ask Ted.

"He is usually working at Jacksonville International," said Ted.

"That's good too," said Bonnie, "I think that is where we will be keeping the Beechcraft, we have an appointment here monday morning and then the plans are to fly over to Jacksonville in the afternoon."

"Alright, I'll make a final check and top off the fuel tanks, she will be ready when you are," Ted concluded.

Bonnie turned to Cindy, "we may as well go back to the hotel, I called Raymond, he is not in but I told his secretary we were back and I would see him monday morning and we could go over what we will say to NASA."

"O.K." said Cindy as they turned and started for the company car.

The drive back to the company garage was quiet and the sun had set and with the clouds that now covered Houston, it was growing dark. they parked the car and started the walk back to the hotel, Bonnie asked, "what are you in the mood for, for dinner?"

"Anything good, I'm hungry," answered Cindy.

"Yes that about covers it," said Bonnie. "let's go freshen up and I will meet you in the lobby."

Bonnie stood waiting as Cindy hurried across the lobby from the elevator, "we know what the food is like here, do you want to go back to the garage and get the car, I know a good restaurant that was recommended," Bonnie said.

"Sure, I'm wide open, I don't know much about the city, the main reason I came here was because Crane Industries had the Beechcraft and I was looking for a job."

"This restaurant was recommended and Neil and I went there just before he left, it's pretty good." Bonnie said.

"You know when i hear you talk about Neil, I think you must have had a very good relationship." Cindy said.

"Yes we did.., I'm in love with him." Bonnie answered.

"Wow that must be tough.., I mean everyone you talk to about him is skeptical, and now that he's gone, you just have to believe he's coming back, and you don't know when," Cindy explained.

"Yes that's about it," Bonnie said.

"How are you going to explain it to the head of NASA?"

"I don't know, Neil is supposed to contact him, and I know Neil is very convincing eye to eye but if he can convince him on a radio or other communication equipment, I just don't know, what I do know is we have got to go over to NASA give them the story and hope we can convince them the story is true." Bonnie explained.

They arrived at the garage and took the Mercedes again and Bonnie drove to the restaurant. "I want to get to sleep so I am going to order ice tea, how about you? "Tea is good," said Cindy.

They enjoyed a good dinner and were soon back at the hotel. "I have got to get eight hours sleep for Monday said Bonnie.

"Yes I can use eight hours myself," said Cindy, "Do you want to have breakfast here in the morning, the hotel restaurant will probably be open by eight."

They ask the desk when the restaurant opened and left a wake up call for 6 O'Clock, then Bonnie had a thought and called the company, the operator said Crane's cafeteria would not be open on Sunday.

Bonnie turned to Cindy, "the company's cafeteria is closed on Sunday and all the people at the hanger will probably be off except for a guard, Why don't we eat here and relax, and then use the lobby to go over the presentation we made in Tallahassee, I am sure there will be more presentations and we can see how we can improve what we have."

"That sounds good," said Cindy, "and then Monday morning I'll go out and check with Ted and make sure the Beechcraft Jet has everything it needs and is ready to fly to Jacksonville."

"Good," said Bonnie," "and I will ask Mr. Crane if he wants to hire an A&E mechanic or just hire one as we need to."

They walked to the elevator and parted on their floor.

"O.K., 7 O'clock it is," said Cindy as she turned for her room.

At 8 O'clock they were in the hotel cafeteria for breakfast and talking about the Beechcraft, "the best thing of course would be to somehow retain a mechanic so he was with Crane Industries and felt a responsibility to the company." Cindy explained.

"Yes that's right," said Bonnie.

They remained in the lobby until lunch time, relaxing and going over the Tallahassee presentation and talking about the Cessna Jet. They went out for lunch and returned to the lobby for the afternoon.

The afternoon was spent relaxing again and going over the Beechcraft jet and it's operating procedures. The lobby had an adjoining room where they could watch the videos of the high speed rail and their Tallahassee presentation.

Bonny glanced at her watch, "well it's getting late what do you say about dinner, Neil and I had a good sea food dinner just before he left, do you want to try it?"

"Yes, sounds good, said Cindy.

They got into the Mercedes again and drove out to the sea food restaurant Bonny and Neil had dinner at before Neil left. They had a leisure dinner and took their time returning the Mercedes and walking back to the hotel.

"That was a good dinner," said Cindy.

"Yes it was," answered Bonny, "and now I need another good nights sleep before I meet NASA in the morning, what do you say we have breakfast at the company restaurant in the morning and maybe we can catch Mr, Crane there?"

"O.K., sounds good to me." said Cindy

They finished breakfast and saw no sign of Raymond Crane it was almost 8:30. "I don't know how we will get to NASA'S headquarters," said bonnie, "Let's go talk to Mr. Crane's secretary."

They walked into Mr. Crane's office and stood at the secretary's desk, she had just arrived. "Oh, good morning, I was about to call you, Mr. Crane will be here any minute," said the secretary as she indicated they take a seat.

"Good morning Ladies," said Mr. Crane as he walked in the door.

"Good morning," the smiling ladies answered.

"Miss Bonnie are you ready to try to convince NASA you know what you are talking about?" Raymond ask.

"I hope so, I think Neil will need his cooperation when he gets back.

Raymond looked over at Cindy, "How are you this morning Cindy?"

"I'm fine," said Cindy, "I need to get out to the airport to talk with Ted and make sure the Hawker Beechcraft is up and ready to go."

"Well that should be easy enough to do," Raymond said, looking at Cindy with a smile.

"I know you have an appointment with NASA this morning and if there is anything I can do, I'm willing." Cindy answered with a smile.

"How about it Bonnie, are we ready to go over and convince NASA.., convince them we have had an extraterrestrial among us and he left and he is coming back and we need to prepare a landing place for him?" said Raymond.

"I sure wish we had something concrete to point to but short of that I guess I am about as ready as I will be," Bonnie answered.

"O.K., Ladies let me check something in my office and then we will be on our way, he started towards his office then stopped turned to his secretary and said, "call the garage and have a limousine brought downstairs," this was a frequent request and the secretary knew exactly what to do.

Bonnie, Cindy and Raymond were soon in the elevator on their way downstairs, "we will drop you off at the field," said Raymond looking at Cindy, "unless you have something you could say that would help convince NASA?"

"No, no, I'm very respectful of NASA and I cain't think of a thing I could say that would convince them." Cindy answered.

Raymond nodded his head in answer and the elevator pinged they were on the ground floor.

The limousine was out front and they all three got in the back, "take us out to the airfield and then we want to go to NASA headquarters, you know the quickest way there don't you?" Raymond asked.

"Yes sir." said the driver as he eased away from the curb.

The conversation was held to a minimum as they made their way to the airfield, each one concentrating on what they were about to do. They arrived at the field and as Cindy got out of the car, Raymond said, "Cindy just plan on flying back to Jacksonville unless something happens in this interview that I can not foresee."

"Yes sir, I will," answered Cindy, she closed the door and the limousine left for NASA headquarters.

It was just before 10 Am, Bonnie and Raymond stood at the desk of the secretary for the head of NASA, Raymond spoke to the secretary, "Yes, my secretary made an appointment for this morning at ten," the secretary was searching her log, "Oh yes, Mr. Crane.., Mr. Hoffman will see you now," she got to her feet and led them to another door and tapped softly, paused a moment and then opened the door, Mr. crane to see you. The head of NASA was sitting at his desk, he looked up at his secretary and got to his feet extending his hand, "Mr. Crane we haven't met but I have heard a lot about you from the media..."

"Yes, well we can not escape that..," Raymond chuckled as he extended his hand, "you probably have had some experience with that."

"Yes I have," said Mr. Hoffman, "and who is this Lady," he ask as he turned towards Bonnie.

"This is Miss Bonnie Steward, she has had most of the personal experience in this matter, she knows more then anyone else..,"

Bonnie extended her hand, Mr. Hoffman took her hand and then said," here take a seat," he indicated the chairs in front of his desk.

They all three settled in their seats.

"Mr. Hoffman, as I said, Bonnie here has a lot of personal experience so I will let her tell you the story."

Bonnie nodded at Raymond and smiled then turned back to Mr. Hoffman,

"Mr. Hoffman you mentioned the media so I will assume you know about the new electric motor Crane Industries just presented to the public..,"

"Yes, yes I watched it on television." He answered.

"Mr. Hoffman that new electric motor and new battery concept was given to Crane Industries by an alien, an extraterrestrial, a man from another planet."

Bonnie had Mr. Hoffman's attention before she said that and now, he sat straight in his chair and blink and then he gave her full eye contact. Bonnie paused a moment and then continued, she started in the desert where she first met Neil and continued right up to the Crane hanger and the airfield and her listening to Neil as he held her and then he got into the ship and took off.

Mr. Hoffman sat back in his chair and then leaned forward and began to speak and gesture with his hands, "you mean to tell me that with Peru's ground based telescopes and then come up to the California mountains and their ground based telescopes, then go to the Hawaiian islands and their ground based telescopes, and the Hubble and James Webb space telescopes and the International Space Station and I don't know how many CIA satellites and the military and then there is the European Space Agency, and don't forget China and Russia, with all of that, you are telling me an alien space ship forced landed here in the desert, the Alien contacted you and you helped him get fuel and another ship came and they repaired the original ship and took off again and six weeks later the original ship landed again and contacted you and then you and the Alien contacted Mr. Crane and flew the space ship to Mr. Crane's hanger in the dead of night and the control tower thought it was a helicopter because they could not see it in the darkness and then the Alien proceeded to design the new electric motor and the new improved batteries and gave it to Crane Industries, then took off again but he's coming back and he will contact me and I need to give him a landing spot at Cape Canaveral."

Mr. Hoffman stopped speaking and looked into the eyes, first of Bonnie's and then Mr. Crane's, there was a pause of silence.

"It's a pretty fantastic story, we know that, said Mr. Crane, "but you will have to meet this Alien as we are calling him, his name is Neil Conrad and he speaks perfect english he looks just like you and me, he could walk into your office here with a question and you would never guess he is from another planet, and yet as you talk to him you are slowly taken by him, he has a sense of authority and as he speaks, you may not agree with him but he speaks with an authority and you know he's right."

"Well.., 'huh' well I..," Mr. Hoffman was hesitant.

"Let me say," said Raymond, you remember a few years ago when that meteor came in here and hit Russia, they said it was doing 40,000 miles per hour when it hit the atmosphere, the light came first and everybody ask what was that and rushed to the windows, the impact was next and it injured about 1600 people, but the point is that meteor came in here and nobody knew about it until it hit, they say it was because it came in low on the horizon rather then a direct hit."

"Yes, yes, I remember that," said Mr. Hoffman.

There was a pause of silence.., "Mr. Hoffman, nobody was more of a skeptic then I was when I first heard this story, I watched Neil design the new electric motor and the new batteries and I was still a skeptic, after talking with him and having dinner with him, I remained a skeptic until he flew his space ship into our airfield and stored it in our hanger. It looks something like the Air force's F-117 only a lot bigger and it is just a small reconnaissance ship, Neil was assigned the job of reconnaissance of our planet, and it wasn't until I saw the ship that I was convinced of the truth of this story," Raymond explained.

"Alright, what is it exactly, that you want me to do?" Said Mr. Hoffman.

"Huh.., not much really.., all we want you to do is accept his message when it comes, we," Raymond indicated Bonnie, "are not sure what he wants, he said his planet is about 700 years ahead of earth's technology and he wants to bring earth up to parr with that.., what he want's you to do, I think, is acknowledge him and then he will tell you what he needs."

Raymond sat silent for a moment, Mr. Hoffman sat thinking, "O.K. then you want me to acknowledge him and accept him when he calls," said Mr. Hoffman.

"Yes, that's basically it," said Raymond, "I think he is trying to get a safe landing and then we will see what he has, if he offers what he did when I met him we are sure to receive for more then we think."

"He said they need us as allies and they are willing to help advance our technology as we do that," said Bonnie, "he says we have dangerous enemies out there that we don't even know about."

There was silent contemplation by all three as they thought about what had just been said.

"O.K.., alright.., I will acknowledge him if he calls me and I will set up a safe landing for him at Cape Canaveral and we will just have to wait and see what happens."

With that said, Mr. Hoffman started to stand at his desk, Raymond and Bonnie stood, they shook hands, and as Raymond and Bonnie started to walk out of the room, Raymond turned and said, "If I hear anything at all, I'll get in touch."

"Good, I don't know if he will call here but if he does, I'll get in touch with Crane Industries, they both nodded in agreement and Bonnie and Raymond walked out of the office.

Mr. Hoffman sat at his desk for sometime thinking about what had just been said, he thought about contacting the CIA, and then the defense department, and then the military.., but what could he say, just repeat what he just heard, he could not prove any of that, it was just hear say, what was he going to do, go around the government repeating rumors, Raymond Crane of Crane Industries was a reputable man with a respected back ground, but to say, he said, was not something you go to the head of government agencies with...

Bonnie and Raymond were in the backseat of the automobile driving back to Crane Industries, "I'm glad you brought up the meteor that struck Russia, I had forgotten about that but I was watching his face and you really got to him with that," Bonnie said.

Raymond looked over at Bonnie and smiled, "good well let's hope he will be ready when Neil calls.

They both sat back in the seat and tried to relax, suddenly Bonnie's cell phone rang, she dug the phone out of her purse and put it to her ear, she sat up on the edge of her seat, "Neil !!" She took the phone from her ear and made sure the sound was as loud as it could be, glanced at Raymond and listened.

"Bonnie, Neil, you can not answer me sweetheart, we just left the vicinity of Mars, we are slowing down, but even so we will be a lot closer to earth by the time you receive this, we don't have the brakes on yet but the propulsion is off, I have five engineers and scientist with me and one of the engineers hooked your cell phone to the ships power, I can call you but you can not call me yet..., I hope someone has talked to the head of NASA and he will accept my call when I make it, when you receive this call, we should be about a week from entering low earth orbit, we have the shield up and we are invisible.., I love you sweetheart and I can barely wait until we can be together..," Neil.

"Did you get that?" Bonnie ask, looking at Raymond.

105

"Yes most of it," said Raymond, he leaned forward and tapped the back of the front seat, "take us back to NASA, hurry, be careful but hurry."

The driver looked for a place to turn around and then they were soon heading back to NASA, he stopped in front of NASA'S headquarters and said, "go ahead in, I'll find a place to park."

Raymond and Bonnie rushed across the entrance to the front door of NASA's headquarters and got on the elevator for Mr. Hoffman's office.

"Is he still in?" Raymond ask the secretary as they walked into her office, she nodded and then pushed an intercom button and ask Mr. Hoffman if he could see them.

She got up walked to the door, tap and open the door, Mr. Hoffman looked up with surprise on his face.

Raymond let Bonnie walk in first, looked at Mr. Hoffman and said, "We just got a cell phone message from Neil, you need to hear this."

Bonnie pulled out the phone set it on the edge of the desk, pressed the on button and made sure the speaker was on loud, she stood back.

Mr. Hoffman sat looking down at the cell phone as Neil's voice began to speak.

The call ended, Mr. Hoffman looked up at Bonnie, "can you play it again?"

Bonnie bent over and pushed the button and Neil's voice came on again.

At the end of the recording, Mr. Hoffman sat there looking at the cell phone in contemplation, after a moment he looked up at Bonnie, "can I have a recording of this?"

"Yes," Bonnie answered.

Mr. Hoffman reached over and pushed the intercom button, "Peggy have Mr. Allen stop what he is doing and come up here."

"Mr. Allen is an engineer in charge of communication for NASA," said Mr. Hoffman. "he should be here any minute."

Mr. Hoffman indicated Bonnie and Raymond should take a seat and he leaned back in his chair thinking.., "well this means we will have an invisible space ship circling planet earth in a week or less," he looked over and made eye contact, first with Bonnie and then Raymond, he got a nod from both and then leaned back thinking.

There was a knock on the door, Peggy open the door and Mr. Allen walked in. Mr. Hoffman got to his feet, "Mr. Allen this is Mr. Crane of Crane Industries and Miss Bonnie Steward.., listen to this," he indicated for Bonnie to turn the recording on.., Mr. Allen stood listening to Neil's voice, at the finish Mr. Hoffman said, "there is a long story here and I don't want to get into it now but will you make a recording of that and get it back here as soon as possible, this Lady needs her cell phone back."

"Yes," said Mr. Allen as he reached for the phone, "I'll be right back."

Mr. Hoffman sat, leaned back and with the door closed he leaned forward, looked at Bonnie and ask, "were you intimate with him?" with..,"

"Yes," answered Bonnie.

"I'm sorry to get so personal, but I am about to give orders that will involve the whole planet," said Mr. Hoffman...

Raymond spoke up, "if Neil walked in here, it would be just like Mr. Allen walking in here, Neil's english is excellent, he looks just like you are me, middle aged, you could place him from London, New York, Toronto, he is an extraterrestrial but you would never guess it."

Mr. Hoffman looked at Raymond, made eye contact and nodded he understood, then he leaned back in contemplation..., "Alright, now what we have to do is contact the World Health Organization, and then the health department in Washington, I'm sure every health department on the planet would want to be there but we have to put a limit on it, I assume from what was said on the recording that they have their shield up and they are invisible and I assume that will hold true until they reach earth orbit so we have got to get everybody on the planet ready so no one will panic when they see a space ship suddenly appear, I'll call Cape Canaveral and get them ready, any other suggestions?"

"No.., no.., Bonnie and I will want to be there but as long as everyone else at least gets the message and as you say they are not suddenly terrified, I think it will be fine." Said Raymond.

There was a soft tap on the door, Peggy opened it and Mr. Allen walked in.

He had Bonnie's cell phone in his hand, unsure what to do with it, he handed it to Bonnie, he started to turn for the door and stopped, he made eye contact with Mr. Hoffman and said, "I have a good copy of that transmission.., it came from deep space."

"How do you know?" Raymond ask.

Mr. Allen turned to Raymond, "I have equipment downstairs that can tell that, It is the only message on the phone that is not local, that is to say not local from here, say Los Angles or El paso, it is definitely from outer space."

Raymond, looking at Mr. Allen nodded yes, he understood.

Mr. Allen looked at everyone then turned for the door.

"O.K., I guess that about covers it for now, I have got to call Washington,

and London, and then Japan, Korea, China, Russia and make sure everyone knows, he started to stand and Bonnie and Raymond stood, call me if you hear anything more," said Mr. Hoffman, "and I will let you know when we have a definite time for the landing."

"O.K.," said Raymond as they shook hands and he and Bonnie turned for the door.

Bonnie and Raymond were in the back seat of the sedan on their way to the airfield, "we have his attention now and his interest, I think he is finally aware how vital this can be for all of us," said Bonnie.

"I think you are right," said Raymond, "with five other engineers and scientist, and a bigger ship, Neil must have some big plans for planet earth."

"And speaking of plans, I got word that a committee is meeting in washington to discuss high speed rail, as soon as Cindy and Ted get the Hawker Beechcraft jet ready, fly back to Jacksonville and wait, the information I have is this committee meeting is similar to the one they had in Florida and if we can get you in there, we need to let them know we have started a high speed rail system here in Florida and we need all the help we can get." Raymond explained.

"Alright I'll do that," said Bonnie.

They arrived at the airfield and Bonnie got out and Raymond told the driver to carry him on to the office.

Bonnie saw the Beechcraft jet was parked out on the apron and the door was open, she walked towards the jet, climbed the steps and stuck her head in the aircraft, "Hello," she said, Cindy was inside doing some last minute cleaning,

"Oh hello," answered Cindy, "you're back, what's the news?"

"We will go back to Jacksonville as soon as the aircraft is ready," said Bonnie.

"O.K. we can go, the fuel tanks have just been topped off, I can file a flight plan and check the weather, we need to get our luggage at the hotel and we can take off," said Cindy.

"O.K., let me see if I can find us a ride to the hotel," said Bonnie, she climbed down the steps and turned for the Hanger, she asked around at the hanger if anyone was going to the office, she found a mechanic who was going into town for lunch and they could have a ride with him.

They checked out of the Hotel and were walking back to the Company garage with their luggage, it was the first time Bonnie had Cindy alone and she began to talk about what happen at NASA.

"You mean Neil called you on your cell when he was out in the vicinity of Mars and he has a space ship with five other engineers and scientist and they expect to land at Cape Canaveral in about a week..,? wow, that will be something." said Cindy

"Yes Mr. Hoffman, the head of NASA was very dubious, and uncertain when Mr. Crane and I got there, and told him about Neil, he said he would wait until Neil called, Mr. Crane and I were in the automobile driving back to the airport when my cell phone rang, it was Neil and he said I could not answer him but he expected to be in low earth orbit in about a week and he would call NASA, we turned around and carried the message back to NASA, at NASA here in Houston, they have an engineer in charge of communication and he has equipment that can tell where the message came from and he said it came from deep space, from the vicinity of Mars.

Mr. Hoffman hearing this finally became interested, Neil's ship has it's shield up and it is invisible and it will repel any missile or space object, but the main thing is Mr. Hoffman will accept Neil's call when it comes and Mr. Hoffman will make accommodations for Neil to land at Cape Canaveral." Bonnie explained.

"Wow," said Cindy.

"And here is the reason we are flying back to JAX," said Bonnie, "Mr. Crane has word there is a committee meeting in washington on high speed rail and he wants to try and get us in there to make a presentation like we did in Tallahassee so we are to sit and wait in Jacksonville until we get word on that and meanwhile Neil is due to start orbiting earth in about a week."

"Sounds like exciting times," said Cindy.

"Yes it is, so now what we have to do is sit in JAX, and see what comes first, the presentation in Washington or Neil starting to orbit earth," said Bonnie.

Bonnie and Cindy walked into the garage and the same driver who drove her and Raymond to NASA headquarters was there, "hello can we get a ride out to the airport?" Bonnie ask.

"Yes are you ready? ask the driver, looking at their luggage. Bonnie and Cindy both nodded yes and then followed him to the automobile.

Seated in the back seat, Bonnie turned to Cindy and ask, "Is there was anything to eat on the jet?"

"No," said Cindy.

"Let's stop and get a couple of take out sandwiches." Cindy nodded and Bonnie leaned forward and ask the driver to stop at a fast food restaurant.

They arrived at the airport and while Cindy went to file the flight plan and check the weather, Bonnie began to load the luggage on the Beechcraft.

Cindy was soon walking towards the Beechcraft jet, she made one final walk around check and climbed the steps and joined Bonnie.

"We should be in the JAX traffic area in a few hours," said Cindy, "do you want to take off?" "That front that was over Houston yesterday has moved off the east coast and we will have high pressure all the way."

"O.K." Said Bonnie, "that sounds good."

They made all the preflight checks then called the tower for permission to taxi, Bonnie in the right seat. Bonnie taxied to the holding area for the main runway, and ran the engines up, "everything checks, you ready?"

She ask Cindy.

"Yes, if I say let me have it, just drop everything," Cindy said looking at Bonnie, Bonnie looked at Cindy and smiled O.K. then called the tower for permission to take off, the tower gave permission, they would climb to twenty six thousand feet and fly to the Jacksonville traffic area.

Bonnie taxied over to the main runway put the front wheel on the center line and started easing the throttles forward and with the throttles at full open and the flaps set for take off the jet quickly left the concrete climbing for 26000 feet, Bonnie occasionally glanced over at Cindy and Cindy glanced back with a nodding grin, They had the fast food on board and in a few hours they flew from Houston to the Jacksonville traffic area, the jet was at top cruising speed and it flew flawlessly all the way.

Bonnie still at the controls, turned the auto pilot off, called JAX for permission to land and began to lose altitude as she flew to the outer marker, at the outer marker she turned for final and lined up on the center line, Cindy followed her every move and grinned when Bonnie glanced over at her.

Bonnie ask for gear down and set the flaps, she came in steady and fast, made a chirp, chirp, landing, second only to the best, 'one chirp,' she pulled the throttles back and glanced over at Cindy, Cindy grinned and said, "go ahead and taxi to the hanger." Bonnie taxied to the hanger and parked the Jet.

"You go close out the flight plan, I'm going to see if I can find this Bill Evans," said Bonnie, she walked into the hanger and began to ask for Bill Evans, a middle aged man walked up, he was dressed in work clothes, slim, brown hair and eyes, "you are looking for Bill Evans?" he asked.

Bonnie turned and made eye contact, "Yes, I just parked that Hawker-Beechcraft," She nodded in the direction of the aircraft, "we flew in here from Houston and Ted Bishop, do you know him?" Evans nodded his head holding eye contact, "He recommend you as a good A&E who knows the Beechcraft jet, so I guess my first question is are you open for employment by Crane Industries?"

A slow grin started to appear on Bill's face, "yes I know Ted, he's a good man, and I could be open for employment, what kind of employment is Crane Industries thinking about?"

111

Bonnie dropped her head thinking, she looked up making eye contact again "Crane Industries is building a high-speed rail system, the north south line, from Miami to Jacksonville will terminate here and then they will cross the country to San Diego and the west east line will terminate here.., so Jacksonville will become important for the High-Speed rail system, we are setting up an office here and we will be doing a lot of travel, a lot of flying, out of Jacksonville and we need a good A&E engineer to look after the Beechcraft jet." Bonnie paused for a moment, letting this sink in.

"Mmmm, that sounds interesting," said Bill, "will you have hanger space here?"

"Yes, we hope too.., huh, Cindy Collins is the chief pilot for the Beechcraft, she is over closing out our flight plan from Houston, why don't you get with her and find out about a convenient hanger space and if you have a piece of paper, I'll give you a phone number to call."

Bill pulled out a business card and gave her the back of it, Bonnie wrote the number down and Alice Wood's name and handed it back to him, "this is Raymond Cranes personal secretary, she knows all about this and she can answer just about any questions you may have.

"Oh here comes Cindy now," said Bonnie as she glanced at the door, "Cindy this is Bill Evans," Cindy offered her hand, "Ted Bishop said a lot of good things about you," said Cindy. "O.K., I was just telling Bonnie here, Ted is a good man, we worked together in St.Louis, that's where I learned the Beechcraft and then Ted went to Houston and I came here, Bill explained.

"Do you own this hanger?" ask Bonnie.

"Oh no, I just work out of here, this hanger is owned by a company here in Jacksonville," Bill explained.

"O.K., good," said Cindy, "well is there a good spot, a corner here in the hanger that you could pull the Beechcraft in out of the cold and check her out, Ted checked it out before we left Houston and we had an almost perfect flight over here, but look it over, we may have to fly to Washington."

"Right, I can handle that," said Bill.

"And when you are ready you can call Alice Wood and talk to her about becoming a member of Crane Industries, you might even talk to Raymond Crane, I think we would be glad to have you," Bonnie said.

"Sounds good to me, this high-speed rail system might change a lot of things, and it would be interesting to be part of it." said Bill.

"Yes it would," said Bonnie, "and now Cindy and I need to go to the office and get ready for a presentation."

Cindy drove the rental car to the office, "He seems O.K., if we can get him on the Crane Industries pay roll, I think he will take care of the Beechcraft," said Bonnie, sitting in the passenger seat.

"Yes, I think so," answered Cindy, keeping her eyes on the road.

At the office, Bonnie found a load of mail and messages, Patricia Wells, Bonnie's secretary was taking care of the office but she could not answer all of the mail, so it just piled up. It was too late in the day to do much so she had Cindy take the luggage to the hotel and she and Patricia worked until almost closing time, and the phone rang.

It was Raymond, "hello.., there you are, I wasn't sure I would find you, how was the trip over?"

"Fine.., fine," said Bonnie, "the Beechcraft was flawless and it really is a luxury to fly."

"O.K., that's good to hear, said Raymond.., "the reason I called, that committee on transportation in Washington is meeting and my man there has made an appointment for you to make a presentation on Thursday afternoon at 2 pm.., they will probably have a late lunch and you will come in right after that, do you think you can make it?"

"Yes I think so," said Bonnie, "we can make about the same presentation we made here in Tallahassee only it will be improved on somewhat.

"O.K. good, our man in Washington is Clarence Bradley, here is his phone number," Raymond gave Bonnie the phone number, and said, "He can take care of just about any problem you may run into up there, so call him in the morning and make the arrangements."

"I will, how are things there have you heard from Hoffman or NASA."

"No everything is pretty quite," said Raymond.

"Yes it's early yet, we probably wont hear anything until Friday, or the weekend," said Bonnie.

"I agree," said Raymond, "O.K. if you run into any kind of major problems and you cain't find me, call my secretary Alice Wood."

113

"I will and I will let you know if there are any major happenings. oh and by the way, I met Bill Evans, he is the A&E mechanic Ted recommended here in Jacksonville, I like him, he seems to know his stuff, and he is taking care of the Beechcraft now and I told him to call Alice Wood about employment with Crane Industries when he is ready."

"Good, I'll mention it to Alice so she will be ready," said Raymond.

Bonnie hung up and turned to Patricia, "well that was Mr. Crane, he tells me there is a committee on transportation meeting on Thursday and he wants Cindy and me there to make a presentation on the Mag-Lev train.., Patricia.., can I call you Pat?"

"Yes please," said Patricia.

"Pat this mail keeps piling up and after this committee meeting it will be piling up even more and I think we need a standard Crane Industries response and all the important letters that require a special response and a signature from Crane Industries, hold them aside until I can get to them, can you do that?"

"Yes, I can handle that." said Pat.

"Good," said Bonnie, "now Cindy and I are going to get together and work on this committee hearing meeting, so take any calls that come in."

"Yes I will," said Pat.

"O.K., well it's time for you to go home, Cindy and I will get the equipment we had in Tallahassee and work on it here, we'll see you in the morning."

"Alright," said Pat as she began to arrange everything for the evening, she took her purse and walked out the door, saying, "good evening."

Bonnie got on her cell phone and called Cindy at he hotel, "Oh hi, I was about to call you," said Cindy.

"I've been busy here, Mr. crane called and they have an appointment for us in Washington on thursday afternoon at 2 O'clock, I told him we could do it and it would be about the same as the presentation we made in Tallahassee but with some improvements, he was pleased with that, so why don't you bring the presentation we made in Tallahassee and we can go over it here?"

"Alright, I'll be right over." Cindy answered.

Cindy arrived with some of the gear and equipment they had in Tallahassee and they began to rewrite the presentation they would use in Washington, they worked into the evening and finally broke for dinner.

As they left the restaurant to walk back to the hotel Bonnie said, "Mr. Crane was O.K. with the hiring of Bill Evans, so if he calls Peggy, he will probably become a member of Crane Industries."

"I think that will be good," said Cindy.

"Yes," said Bonnie, "We have a man in Washington.., Clarence Bradley, we can call him and get any help we need, I think I will call him in the morning and let him get us a hotel and we can fly up on Wednesday afternoon, and spend Thursday morning getting ready for the presentation, you get with Bill Evans and make sure the Beechcraft is ready to go on Wednesday."

"O.K., and I can file the flight plan and start to get the gear we will need and put it on the Beechcraft."

"O.K., good," said Bonnie.

The next morning FED EX had a package at the office, it was from Ben Hadley, Crane Industries head of advertising, he sent over brochures and a new video of a Mag-Lev train in China, it was good and Bonnie could use it in her new presentation.

She and Cindy spent the day rewriting the presentation and getting everything ready to take to Washington, finally Bonnie had Cindy take the equipment they would need for the presentation out to the airport and check with Bill Evans and make sure the Beechcraft was checked out and ready to go the next day, Bonnie stayed at the office and worked with Pat on the mail. Cindy returned to the office, Pat had left for the day, Cindy began to help with the final preparations for the presentation in Washington.

Finally they broke for dinner and picked a nearby restaurant. They sat across from each other, "Bill is doing a good job with the Beechcraft, he has it inside and he has been polishing it and it really looks good," said Cindy, "I didn't ask him about coming to work for Crane Industries yet but he has checked out the Mag-Lev and he is very interested in that and I think he is working with some of the people he is contracted with and I think once he gets it settled he will be calling Houston.

"Good that will be one problem solved if he does," said Bonnie, "we need to get a good nights sleep, I called Clarence Bradley, he has made hotel reservations for us and we need to finish up on the presentation and fly up to Washington tomorrow morning and get everything ready for the presentation, are you ready to go?"

"Yes, I put all the audio and video tapes and charts on the Jet and I'm sure Bill has it ready to fly so we can use tomorrow to fly to DC, check in and do whatever we need to be ready for the presentation." comments Cindy.

"Alright then what is needed is a good nights sleep," said Bonnie as they pay for the dinner and turn to go back to the hotel.

The next morning they have a good breakfast and return to the office and do some last minute work and check with Pat that everything is O.K. They drive the rental to the airport and Cindy checks with Bill while Bonnie gets the luggage on board and they are ready to fly. Cindy lets Bonnie take off and plans to take control when they enter the DC traffic area.

The Hawker Beechcraft jet performed flawlessly again, Cindy took control as they entered the Washington DC traffic area, She called and asked for permission to land at the municipal air field, she was given the outer marker, she flew there and lined up for final approach. Cindy put the Hawker Beechcraft jet on the concrete with one chirp and turned for the hanger. At the hanger Cindy secured the jet and closed out her flight plan, Bonnie found a phone in the hanger and called Clarence Bradley and told him they had arrived and were going to check into the hotel, he advised her on where the committee would be meeting and she could set up while they were out for lunch.

Bonnie and Cindy hired a rental and carried the equipment and luggage to the hotel.

They had a good dinner and turned in early to get a good start in the morning.

The next morning they found a good place for breakfast and Bonnie called Clarence and checked with him on when the committee usually breaks for lunch, She told him what she had and he advised her how to set it up and said he would be there and help any way he could.

At lunch time they were in an adjoining room and watched as the committee broke for lunch, Clarence help them set up as soon as the room was mostly clear.

They had the equipment and props set up and were ready to go as the committee began to filter back in after lunch.

Bonnie had the confidence she had in Tallahassee and with Cindy helping with the props, she gave the committee what they wanted to hear about High Speed Rail and she held Mag-Lev until the end, she had Cindy put the videos of the Mag-Lev trains from China, Germany and Japan on the screen, she started with the initial cost would be high but she made the point there would be no pollution, it would be easy to maintain once it was set up and the cost to operate would be unbelievable compared to other High Speed rail systems.

Bonnie and Cindy did not go to lunch as they did in Tallahassee, but they took down the biggest charts and left the committee room and let the committee discuss what they had just heard.

Bonnie and Cindy returned from coffee and found the committee room was emptying, they could not find Clarence, he apparently was taking care of other business, they began to pack up their equipment and took it down to the car rental.

"Well what do you think, should we try to fly back to Jacksonville tonight or go back to the hotel," Bonnie ask.

"We can fly at night, that's no problem," said Cindy, "I just wonder if we wouldn't feel better tomorrow if we stayed in the hotel to night?"

"I think we would feel better with a good nights sleep," said Bonnie."We can take this equipment out to the airport and load it on the plane and come back to the hotel, we would have to do that anyway," comments Cindy.

They take the presentation equipment out to the airport and load it on the Beechcraft, it was getting dark by the time they start back to the hotel, they decide to find a good restaurant for dinner and then go back to the hotel and get an early start for the flight back to Jacksonville.

Cindy is driving and Bonnie sits next to her in the front seat, suddenly Bonnie's phone begins to ring, she hauls her purse up on the seat and begins to search for the cell phone. "hello?"

"Bonnie! Raymond here, you and Cindy did it again, Washington is interested in High-Speed Rail and they were interested to learn someone had started on one, and they were very interested in Mag-Lev, Clarence was there and he circulated among the committee and talked to them after you left.., I believe you sold them on Mag-Lev, the big problem is, they don't know how much it cost so I'm going to get Crane Industries Legal Department to get in touch with the committee and see if we can get Washington interested in investing in Mag-Lev."

"Good, I mentioned that it would be expensive but I didn't say how much, so the legal department will not be able to surprise them." said Bonnie.

"Good, that's good," said Raymond, "if we can get some government help with a mag-lev on the east coast of Florida from Miami to Jacksonville,

and it is successful, the run over to San Diego from Jacksonville should be a lot easier."

"I think so," said Bonnie," not only will it be easier to finance, everybody will want it."

"Yes." said Raymond.

"Are you going to fly back to Jacksonville tonight?" Raymond ask.

"No, we have decided to get a good nights sleep here and get an early start for Jacksonville in the morning." explained Bonnie.

"That's probably the best," said Raymond.

"Yes, huh.., have you heard anything from Houston or NASA?"

"No if they are doing anything, they are keeping it pretty quiet." Explained Raymond.

"That's better then letting the media know, I can just imagine what they would do with that news," said Bonnie.

"Yes," said Raymond.

"Patricia is taking care of the Jacksonville office and that mail keeps piling up, I've ask her to make a standard response letter and anything she thinks needs a personal response and signature, I will handle." said Bonnie.

"Good, call Alice at least once a day, if I'm not there she will know where I am and she can probably handle most problems." said Raymond.

"Alright I will," said Bonnie, "we are driving back from the airport now and we expect to have dinner then turn in and get an early start in the morning and we expect to be in Jacksonville by noon."

"Good," said Raymond, "call us when you get there and tell Cindy she did a very good job.., Goodbye." Raymond clicked off.

"Did you get that?" Bonnie turned to Cindy?

"Yes most of it," she said without taking her eyes off the traffic.

"O.K. well let's go back to the hotel and see if they can recommend a good place to eat.

They parked the rental car and checked with the desk at the hotel and they recommended a close by restaurant.

Cindy and Bonnie sat across from each other, the waiter had just taken their order. "that was good news from Mr. Crane," said Bonnie, "we really need to get that Mag-Lev built, if they build a line from Tampa through Orlando and have a connection at Daytona Beach, that would mean even with a stop at Daytona Beach they could make a run from Jacksonville down to Miami in less then two hours and there would be no pollution, we really have got to get that done."

"I agree," said Cindy, "just driving here and in Jacksonville, you can see there are to many cars on the streets and highways and not all the drivers are that good at driving and the ones that are good tend to let their cell phones get in the way."

"Yes you are right," said Bonnie, "and add the carbon monoxide that is pouring into the atmosphere, something has got to be done and I think we are fast getting to the point where it may be too late." The waiter interrupted with the ice tea.

"It's chilling just to think about," said Cindy.

"Yes it is," agreed Bonnie.

They finished the dinner and returned to the hotel and left an early wake-up call at the desk and turned in.

The next morning they arrived at the airport just before first light, Bonnie returned the automobile rental while Cindy filed the flight plan and had the Beechcraft pulled out onto the apron. Bonnie returned with a tray of coffee and sandwiches and they climbed aboard the Beechcraft. While Cindy sipped the coffee and ran the preflight checks, Bonnie sat watching.

Finally just as the sun was breaking the horizon, Cindy fired both engines and pulled over to the holding area, she ran the engines up and called the tower for permission to take off, permission was granted, and Cindy looked over at Bonnie and ask, "You want to take off?"

"Yes,"

Bonnie took the controls and pulled over onto the runway, with the front wheel on the center line she glanced at Cindy, "you ready?"

"Yes,"

Bonnie pushed both throttles forward and the Beechcraft began to move,

gaining speed, with the Beechcraft straining, shuddering to leave the concrete, Bonnie eased the yoke back, the Beechcraft left the concrete and smoothed out, "Gear up," said Bonnie, the flaps were set for climbing, they were heading for 30000 feet.

"Good, that was good," said Cindy, "I'll set the auto pilot for 30000 feet and the Jacksonville outer marker.

The Beechcraft will be flown by the auto pilot now, Bonnie eased off the controls and sat observing the instruments.

The flight to Jacksonville's outer marker was flawless Cindy called Jacksonville's control for permission to land, permission was granted and Cindy turned off the auto pilot and began to loose altitude and speed, she turned for final approach at the outer marker and lined up for the landing. It was a one chirp almost perfect landing, she taxied over to the hanger and parked.

Cindy went to close her flight plan, Bonnie got the car rental and began to unload the equipment, Bill Evans came out and Cindy turned the Beechcraft over to him and She and Bonnie got into the car and drove back to the office.

"I guess Bill hasn't called Houston yet, I didn't bother to ask, I figure he will say so when he decides what he wants to do," said Bonnie.

"I think so," said Cindy in the right seat.

At the office they unloaded the equipment and then found a good place for lunch, back at the office, Cindy made herself useful taking care of the videos and other equipment and Bonnie gathered up the pile of mail and she and Pat were well into clearing it up by mid afternoon.

Eric Hoffman over at NASA had been busy all day calling the space agencies all across the planet, he was mainly just checking in to see how everyone was doing and he did not mention Raymond and Bonnie's visits yet. He sat there in his office thinking about the visit and he realized how difficult it would be for him to do the same thing. He thought how a man of Raymond Crane's stature walking into his office with a cock and bull story like that made no senses, and he realized it must be true.

As Eric Hoffman sat there, suddenly his telephone rang, he reached over and picked it up, "hello?"

"Hello, is this Eric Hoffman, of NASA?"

"Yes it is," answered Eric.

"Mr. Hoffman, this is Neil Conrad, has someone talk to you about me?"

There was a moment of silence and Mr. Hoffman spoke, "Yes, Raymond Crane of Crane Industries and Bonnie Steward, came here and spoke of you."

"That's fine then you know who I am?" said Neil.

"Yes, I Think so," said Mr. Hoffman.

"Mr. Hoffman, I'm on a space ship with five other scientist and engineers,

we have been slowing down since we left the vicinity of Mars, we are about to orbit earth, I figure we will orbit your planet three or four times in order to slow enough to land, we have our shield up and you can not see us and it would take an extraordinary weapon to penetrate our shield. we will not collide with any satellites.., we may push one out of the way, especially some of your micro-satellites.., Mr. Hoffman we need permission to land at Cape Canaveral.

"Well.., huh, Mr. Crane said you would be calling, and to be completely frank and candid, I have been reluctant to believe this story.., I have had NASA telescopes, the CIA and anybody else I could think of who would keep their mouths shut to look and see if you were out there and you are right, you can not be seen."

"Mr. Hoffman, the fact that you talked to people who can keep their mouths shut is a good thing, if we can keep the heads of government out of this until we can get established it will be a good thing..., I have the brain power on board that can build a deep space penetrating ship, but it will take the cooperation of all of planet earth and the biggest problem we will have will be politics."

"Yes politics will be a problem alright," said Mr. Hoffman.

"Mr. Hoffman, you probably already know this, but I think it bears repeating, the amazon river valley has been referred to as the lungs of Planet Earth, the trees and plants there are essential to the health of Planet Earth and the life on it, and yet there are people who are cutting down the jungle and planting crops, they can not afford fertilizer so they get one or two crops and then they move on and start all over again, there is a land locked country down there that has cut all the trees right down to the top soil and they are in hopes of getting commercial farming, Agra-Business in there to plant crops and give their people employment..., Mr. Hoffman this will not work and in addition to that, they are building automobiles world wide and the power companies are filling the atmosphere with carbon monoxide, burning fossil fuel to produce the energy to build the automobiles and then the automobiles are poured out onto the streets and highway burning more fossil fuel to power the engines..., this not only will not work, but it is just a matter of time before Planet Earth starts to die from carbon monoxide.

"Yes, I know this," said Mr. Hoffman, "and you talk to the power companies and they will tell you give us a little more time and we will stop burning fossil fuels and convert to none fossil fuels for the power and the automobile companies will tell you, give us a little more time and we will build electric automobiles."

"Yes, I know, when it comes to building wealth it is very difficult to get someone to stop or change their methods," said Neil, "and it is very difficult to get people to invest in the future of the planet with such things as High Speed rail using Magnet-Levitation..."

"It's because the cost is very high," said Mr. Hoffman, "I think they would rather invest in welfare because they can put their name on it and there is no chance of a loss." Mr. Hoffman explained.

"That's true," said Neil, "Mr. Hoffman I'm glad to see we are in agreement on our thinking, we are approaching earth orbit and we are still slowing down and in a few hours we will orbit earth two or three times and then we will enter low earth orbit and I will keep the shield up to avoid any satellites,

but I need permission to land at Cape Canaveral.

"I think I can get you in there," said Hoffman.

"Good," said Neil, "and Mr. Hoffman if we can keep the individual governments out of this until we get established, it will run a lot smoother, I know the United Nations is not as powerful as they could be, but maybe you could get the World Health Organization to Cape Canaveral as a reception committee, it would offer some relief and make a lot of people happy."

"Yes, I think I can do that," said Hoffman.

"Good.., well we are getting close to Earth now and I have to get back to the instruments, can I call you back when I am ready to orbit Earth?"

"Yes," answered Mr. Hoffman.

"Alright, will do," said Neal as he signed off.

Mr. Hoffman sat there at his desk in silence..., "What have I done?" he thought.., he reached for the phone and dialed the White House, he could not reach the President immediately and finally he got in contact with the president's adviser for the defense department, He started with Raymond and Bonnie's visit and made the point of how skeptical he was with the whole story and how he used NASA telescopes and the CIA and anybody else he could think of who would keep their mouths shut and nobody could find a trace of the space ship and then when Neil called Earth, called him on his phone, he finally conceded there must be some truth here.

"No, no," continued Mr. Hoffman, "as long as they have the shield up, you can not see them and I am pretty confident we do not have a weapon that will penetrate that shield if we wanted to.., I talked to Miss Bonnie Stewart, the woman who came with Raymond Crane, and she readily admitted to being intimate with Neil Conrad, the man who called me and there has been enough time now that if there was any danger of contamination it would have shown itself and she is about as beautiful a young woman as you would want to find..," Mr. Hoffman explained.

There was a pause of silent thinking and Mr. Hoffman spoke, "I think they are completely benign and I think they are exactly what they say they are, they want to advance our technology about one thousand years and they need us as an ally."

"Mmm, you say it is a matter of hours before they begin to orbit the Planet?"

"Yes," answered Mr. Hoffman.

"O.K. I'll advise the president," said the defense advisor.

"Good, and I think we should get in touch with The United Nations and get the World Health organization to send a reception committee to Cape Canaveral, it will make everyone feel better and then I think I should get in touch with the heads of all the Planet's space agencies and let them know what's about to happen."

"Yes that sounds good," said the Advisor, "alright let me get with The President."

Mr. Hoffman hung up his phone and called his secretary in and told her to keep the line open in case he got a call then he left his office and went downstairs to the communication room and starting with the British, he called the heads of all the planets space agencies and explained what was about to happen and to relax because there was not much they could do even if they wanted to, then he went back to his office and waited.

Bonnie and Pat finally had the mail just about under control, it was the end of the day and and Pat left for home, Cindy and Bonnie sat contemplating what they would do for dinner, Bonnie's cell range, "hello? Neil!" Bonnie sat up straight in her chair.

"Hello sweetheart, what are you doing? ask Neil.

"I'm sitting here missing you," said Bonnie, "where are you?"

"I am just about to orbit planet Earth, I just got off the phone with the head of NASA, I have permission to land at Cape Canaveral, I calculate we need to orbit three or four times and then drop down to low earth orbit, I will keep the shield up so we will not collied with any of the satellites or space junk in low earth orbit so you can not see us.., I'm on your cell phone and it is still connected to the ship's power but I am a little surprised to see your new cell phone is able to connect it must be some kind of atmosphere phenomenon.

"I hear you just fine," said Bonnie.

"Good, have you talked to Raymond? is he ready to come to Cape Canaveral?" ask Neil.

"I haven't talk to him but I will, when do you think you will land? ask Bonnie.

"I'm pretty sure Cape Canaveral will let us come in like the space Shuttle, I'm calculating some time Sunday Morning."

"Be careful and remember someone here loves you," said Bonnie.

"Alright, sweetheart, I love you too.., now I am going to have to hang up and call Mr. Hoffman And then we will have to talk to Cape Canaveral, you call Raymond Crane and bring him up to date and tell him I expect to see him on Sunday."

"I will, I will, and Neil you be careful." said Bonnie.

"I'm always trying to do that," said Neil, "and you be careful driving."

"I will, I love you Neil," said Bonnie as she punched off, she exhaled and collapsed back into her chair, she looked over at Cindy, "that was Neil, did you get that?"

"Some of it," said Cindy.

"They are still slowing down and they are about to orbit earth, Neil has been talking to the head of NASA and he is about to start talking to Cape Canaveral, after they orbit Earth three or four times, they expect to enter low Earth orbit and then with Cape Canaveral's permission they expect to land sometime Sunday morning..."

"Here, let me call Mr. Crane," she started punching in the number for Crane Industries, Mr. Cranes secretary was preparing to leave for the weekend, she turned and picked up her phone, "Oh hello Bonnie, yes he's in his office, just a second, I'll connect you..."

"Bonnie! where are you, I was about to call you, you and Cindy are building quite a reputation, Washington has been taken with the Mag-Lev idea."

"That's wonderful," said Bonnie, "We are in Jacksonville, and I just got a call from Neil, his cell is connected to the space ship and it has plenty of power, and he was surprised to see my cell phone reaches the ship, he thinks i may be some kind of atmospheric phenomenon, but they are about to orbit earth, they are still slowing down and they have the shield up and will keep it up until they are about to land to avoid satellites and space junk in low Earth orbit, Mr. Hoffman is getting him permission to land at Cape Canaveral, and they will come in like the space shuttle on Sunday morning and Neil said he expects to see you at Cape Canaveral."

There was a slight pause and then Raymond spoke.

"Wow, well I guess we can make that, O.K., I'll fly over to Jacksonville and spend the night and we can fly down to Cape Canaveral and be part of the welcoming committee."

"Good," said Bonnie, "Bill can take care of the Jet, has he called Alice yet, he is doing a super job on the Beechcraft, I didn't ask but I think he is talking with his other clients about making the switch to Crane Industries."

"No I don't think he has, I'll talk to him when I get there."

"O.K., Patricia just left for the weekend and we have just about got the mail under control, we have a standard letter for most of it and Cindy and I are taking care of the mail that needs an individual answer and a signature.., so you are flying over tomorrow and you will spend the night and we will fly down to the Cape early Sunday morning, I'm wondering if we should call Mr. Hoffman over at NASA and be sure we have a welcome on arrival?"

"Yes that's a good idea, let me take care of that." said Raymond.

"Alright, we will be prepared for your arrival tomorrow.

"Right and tell Cindy she did a really impressive job in Washington and I'll see you tomorrow."

"We will look forward to seeing you," and Bonnie click off.

She turned to Cindy, "did you get much of that?

"Some of it," said Cindy.

"He is very impressed with the results of our Washington presentation and he said to tell you, you did a very good job," Cindy sat smiling as she took this in, "apparently we have sold Washington on Mag-Lev high speed rail, the only problem is they have no idea how much it will cost." Bonnie paused, "lets see now," she continued, "Neil will be landing sometime on Sunday Morning and Raymond Crane wants to be there, he is flying over here and will spend the night and hopefully we will all fly down to the Cape and be a reception committee for the space ship when it lands, Mr. Crane is calling Mr. Hoffman over at NASA to be sure we will get in there."

"That should be quite impressive, watching a space ship come in for a landing," said Cindy.

"Yes it will be, especially an alien ship," said Bonnie, "Neil said they will come in very much like the space shuttle."

"Wow that will be an event, you know that will be an event for the twenty first century and even for the history of earth," said Cindy.

"Yes, you are right, I haven't given it a lot of thought but a lot of money and time has been given to the search for other life in the Universe and now here it is about to land at Cape Canaveral." answered Bonnie.

There was a pause as they both gave thought to what had just been said, Bonnie spoke, "we have got to get dinner and then we will need a good nights sleep, we will find out what is in store for us tomorrow when Mr Crane arrives, I suspect they will close off the air space around the Cape, and we will have to be there before they do."

"Yes, I think you are right" said Cindy.

Bonnie picked up her purse, put the phone answering service on and turned to Cindy, "you ready?"

"Yes," said Cindy, they locked the office and walked down to the restaurant they normally used. They read the menu, ordered dinner and sat waiting to be served.

"The few people who know what is about to happen are like us, they have not had time to really think about it.., this really is going to be a historic event," said Bonnie.

"Have you got your cell phone?" ask Cindy.

"Yes," answered Bonnie as she reached over and squeezed her purse, "this is where the information will come in and I am ready."

"All we can do now is wait," said Cindy.

"Yes you are right, when Mr. Crane comes in here tomorrow he will have talked to Mr. Hoffman at NASA and we will know if we will be there or not."

"I guess we had better get a good nights sleep and be prepared for what- ever happens on Sunday, we may have to get up very early." said Cindy.

They walked back to the hotel and left a wake-up call for the desk, Bonnie plugged her cell phone in when she got to her room, and made sure it was charged and ready to go.

Bonnie and Cindy were at breakfast the next morning when Bonnie's cell phone rang, it was Raymond.

"Good morning, I didn't wake you did I?" ask Raymond.

"No, no, we are at breakfast, answered Bonnie.

"O.K., good," said Raymond, "I'm in the air, we just left Houston and we should be there in a couple of hours, I have been in touch with NASA and everything is go, I don't want to talk about it on this phone, so wait until I get there, enjoy your breakfast, take your time and we will plan on being at the Cape on Sunday. Raymond clicked off.

"Woo, did you get that?" Bonnie asked Cindy.

"Well, yes and no," answered Cindy.

"That was Raymond, he is in the air, he just left Houston and he will be here in a couple of hours, he has been talking with NASA and everything is go for Sunday, he did not want to get into details on the phone, he will do that when he gets here meanwhile plan on being at the Cape on Sunday."

Bonnie sat back in her chair, "well that's good news," she smiled at Cindy,

"I haven't said so but I have been very skeptical this was ever going to happen, that is, that Neil would get to land at the Cape Canaveral, When we were talking with Mr. Hoffman over at NASA, when we first gave him the story, I could see in his eyes he didn't believe it and it has taken Mr. Crane and me to finally, maybe get him to start to believe what we were saying, now I guess Neil has convinced him."

"When you first hear that story it is very easy to be skeptical," said Cindy.

"Yes you are right, you have to be around Neil for a while to realize how special he is, after you have been around him for a while and talk to him you realize if he is from this planet, he is very special and then if he tells you who he is and where he is from, it is very easy to believe him." Bonnie explained.

"Well we need to get back to the office and check the mail and get things ready for Mr. Crane when he gets here." Bonnie said, She motioned the waiter over and ask for the bill.

They walked back to the office and spent the morning checking the new mail and sorting the mail they already had and getting the office ready for Raymond when he arrived.

Finally it was a little after noon, Bonnie and Cindy started to discuss lunch and where they would get it and Bonnie's cell range, "Hello?"

"Oh hello, yes we are here in the office, can we come and get you?'

"No I'm on the way, I should be there in a few minutes, have you had lunch?"

"No!" Said Bonnie.

"Good, we can go together.., I don't like talking on this cell phone unless I have to, I'll be there in a minute." Raymond pressed the phone off.

Bonnie pressed her cell off and turned to Cindy, "I guess you know that was Mr. Crane, he's on the way, we will go to lunch together."

Bonnie and Cindy looked up, Raymond was at the door, he had his luggage and as he came in he said, "I called the hotel and made reservation for tonight, I guess I can leave this luggage here while we go to lunch?"

"Yes, let me help you," said Bonnie as she took the bag into the inner office, she returned to the outer office and Mr. Crane looked at them both and said, "you ladies look just fine and you have done a fine job of impressing Washington with High-Speed Rail and Crane Industries and you are right, I talked to Bill out at the airport, he is taking good care of the Beechcraft and he can take care of the Cessna and as soon as he gets the application completed he will be a member of Crane Industries, he's very interested in High-Speed Rail."

He paused for a moment and said, "If you two ladies are ready for lunch, I need the exercise, can we walk over?"

"Sure, that's fine," said Bonnie.

As the three of them walked over to the restaurant for lunch, Raymond began to speak, "I was with Mr. Hoffman over at NASA just before I left Houston, he has notified Washington and he has called all the space agencies around the planet and notified them that an Alien spaceship is landing at Cape Canaveral, I think he is still a bit skeptical and he has manage to not let the media know.., but this is fine and if we can just keep it up it will make everything a lot easier, Neil's ship is in contact with Cape Canaveral's air traffic control and they expect to make a final approach tomorrow shortly after 1:00 pm."

"Bonnie and I have been talking, this is certainly a historical event, not only for Cape Canaveral and NASA, but for the whole planet," said Cindy.

"Yes it is and there is still a lot of skepticism that it is even happening," said Raymond.

They entered the restaurant and found Raymond's favorite table was empty, they sat there and waited for the waiter.

"Mr. Hoffman told me we could have four people at the reception, but we have got to be there before 10 A.M. after that he is closing the Cape down and there will be no air traffic around Cape Canaveral until after the space ship has landed," said Raymond.

He paused from speaking for a moment and then said, "It was just the pilot and I that flew the Cessna over here, I left the pilot at the airfield talking with Bill Evans, they are making sure the Cessna is ready to go in the morning, we could fly the Beechcraft, but the Cessna is bigger and perhaps more impressive, I want to sit in the back with Bonnie and you will have to come and be the co-pilot Cindy."

"Thats great, I really wouldn't want to miss out on this, said Cindy, but you know I am not qualified for the Cessna."

"You can call this a training flight and if we have to, I can use my pilots license and be the co-pilot. we want to take the Cessna because it will have food on board in case we have to eat there."

"That's great because I really want to be there," said Cindy.

"Cindy you are far better qualified then some others I have run into," Raymond said as he looked over at Cindy and Cindy returned a beaming smile.

"O.K., that settles that, now let's see what's for lunch," said Raymond as he reached for the menu.

The waiter returned to the table and stopped in front of Raymond, Raymond looked up, "I'll take number six, the shrimp salad and bring me some unsweetened tea, he turned and said Ladies?"

Bonnie and Cindy ordered and handed over the menus.

Raymond turned to Bonnie, "Bonnie what is your thinking about the people in Washington and the States where you have presented the Meg-Lev high speed rail system?"

"Everyone is very enthusiastic about the idea of a Meg-Lev high-speed rail system that requires little to maintain and is less costly to operate but the big enthusiasm is, there is no pollution.., and I have not gotten into the cost, because I really can't talk about it, I don't know enough about it."

"Yes cost is the big hold up, once you start talking about the cost it just scares everybody off," said Raymond.

"I haven't got any kind of information yet but Neil was very much in favor of Meg-Leg, they have it on his home planet and I am Hoping he will have something that will help us, at least something that will help us hold the cost down," said Bonnie.

"Yes that would be helpful," said Raymond.

The conversation stopped as the waiter began to bring the lunch to the table.

"From what I've seen on the Videos and heard what has been said about it, I believe Meg-Lev would be the answer for High-Speed rail," said Cindy, "even if the cost to build it is very high, when you are finished with it you would have a real treasure."

"That was well said Cindy and that is the point we need to concentrate on and keep repeating.., when the Meg-Lev is finished people will be able to get on the train and go where ever they want to go and not have to worry about driving in this ever increasing automobile traffic and they wont have to worry about the high cost of fuel that is polluting the air we are all trying to breath." Raymond said.

"Yes," said Bonnie, "we need to talk about the cost in our next presentation, we need to keep talking about it until it becomes common knowledge and everyone begins to loose their fear of it, is there any way we can figure out the cost, say the cost per mile?"

"I don't know," said Raymond, "there are so many outside factors such as right of way, some of it will have to be elevated, probably most of it, and then there are the obstacles like rivers and and swamps, I am very hopeful Neil will have some answers for us, he has five other scientist and engineers with him."

"He's bringing a lot with him, I'm sure of that," said Bonnie, "I think planet earth is about to enter a whole new technological era."

"That sounds very exciting," said Cindy.

"It will be," said Bonnie, "but we have got to stop over populating this planet, we have got to make love and not babies, each married couple should have two babies, one to replace the Father and one to replace the Mother, and that's it, this business of having four or five babies because others said so, or someone in authority said so, has got to stop, I was reading a case recently where a mother had twelve children and she was bragging to the media that they were all boys.., now if those boys hold true to their Mother's guidance, in 18 to 20 years that twelve will become one hundred and forty four.., and even if she can support them, there is a limit to the food and air to breath on this planet and each new automobile burning fossil fuel is pumping carbon monoxide into the atmosphere, replacing the oxygen we need to breath."

"You are right of course," said Raymond, "and the problem with trying to change that will be about as complicated and difficult as getting everyone to accept the high cost of Mag-Lev High-Speed Rail."

They continued to finish the luncheon and Raymond spoke, "well ladies, I need to make some phone calls, if you are ready I guess we can go back to the office."

"Yes, Cindy and I can work on the mail some more," said Bonnie.

They took a slow walk back to the office and Raymond entered the inner office and began to make phone calls, after about an hour a man came to the door and ask, "Is this Crane Industries and is Mr. Crane here?"

"Yes Are you the Crane Industries pilot?" ask Bonnie.

"Yes" answered the man.

"Come in, we have been expecting you," said Bonnie Raymond hearing the conversation came to the door, "Wayne come in, this is Bonnie and Cindy, Bonnie Steward is the head of public relations for Crane Industries and Cindy here is the chief pilot for the Beechcraft and she is assisting Bonnie on the PR jobs, ladies this is Wayne Edwards chief pilot for the Cessna.

"How do you do?" ask Wayne.

"So is the Cessna ready to go?" ask Raymond.

"Yes it is, all we have to do is roll it out and it is ready to go were ever you want." said Wayne, "I was with Bill Evans out at the airport, he knows his stuff, he's a good man."

"Yes we are planning on putting him on the pay roll," said Raymond., "Wayne, have you checked into the hotel? I have a few more phone calls to make, would you mind taking this luggage over to the hotel and have them put it in my room and then you need to register and get a room for the night, we will have to get dinner and an early start tomorrow, they will be closing Cape Canaveral down at 10 AM and we have got to get there before that."

"Sure," said Wayne, as he reached for the bag.

"Ladies," said Wayne, as he left the office.

Raymond worked for two more hours then checked with Bonnie and Cindy and they closed the office and walked to the hotel, Raymond checked with the desk and made sure Wayne was checked in and got his room number, he turned to Bonnie and Cindy and said, "can we meet here in about 45 minutes and then go to dinner?" "I'll call Wayne."

"Yes fine," said Cindy and she and Bonnie turned for their rooms.

They all met in the lobby and decided on a place for dinner, they all agreed on Raymond's favorite restaurant, the food was good and it seemed to satisfy everyone.

They were all seated at Raymond's favorite table, "I guess by noon tomorrow, a lot of skepticism will disappear," said Raymond.

"I can understand the skepticism," said Cindy, "If you stop and think about it, we have a space ship from a mother ship that is at another solar system and the space ship is about to land here with six aliens that look and act exactly like us, it answers all the questions we have had about other life in the universe, and we are about to witness it tomorrow."

"Is that what's about to happen?" Wayne ask," he had been told about some of the things going on but he had not been fully briefed.

"Yes didn't you know that?" ask Cindy

"Well I knew there was a space ship trying to get into Cape Canaveral, I did not know it was a space ship from another solar system." explained Wayne.

"Yes," said Raymond, "the pilot has been here on earth twice before and they have their shields up to protect themselves from satellites and space junk, no one can see them and there is a lot of skepticism that they even exist, so we continued to try and convince everybody they were on their way, and everyone was nice enough but they just did not really believe it could be happening, so we just decided to stop talking about it until we had proof."

"Looks like we will have proof in the morning," said Bonnie.

"Yeah, well, I sure don't want to miss that, I was thinking it was a space ship from one of the other nations here on earth, like China or Russia. that was trying to land at Cape Canaveral, but a space ship full of Aliens, well I sure don't want to miss that, what do we have to do to make sure we are there?" Wayne ask.

"Just get up early enough," said Raymond.

"I can do that," Wayne commented.

"O.K. people we need to get dinner and get back to the hotel and turn in, we will have to be landed and secure at the Cape by 9:30 to be sure they will let us in." said Raymond, he looked up and motioned the waiter over.

They finished dinner and returned to the hotel and with a wake up call at 04:00 for everyone, and with agreement to meet in the lobby at 04:30, they all turned in.

Bonnie was the first one in the lobby waiting, soon everyone was there before 04:30, they got into the automobile and started for the airport, Raymond in the back seat with Wayne Comments, "there doesn't seem to be a restaurant open for breakfast.., we can make coffee on the Cessna and there should be Danish and Croissants, I'm wondering if we should call Bill Evans to help us get the Cessna out?"

"If someone is at the hanger and can let us in, I think we can get the Cessna out on the ramp by the time Bill can get there," said Wayne, "What do you think Cindy?"

"Yes, I think so," answered Cindy.

They arrived at the hanger and a night watchman was there, Raymond got out and talk to him, he unlocked the hanger and Wayne open the door and got the tug and began to attach it to the Cessna, Cindy went and flied a flight plan and Bonnie stood and waited until the Cessna was parked on the apron where the jets back blast would not harm anything.

Wayne disconnected the tug from the front gear and returned the tug.

Bonnie started for the Cessna, she climbed aboard and soon had the coffee perking and she was warming the croissants.

Cindy returned with the flight plan, Raymond and Wayne closed the hanger door and started for the Cessna, they all sat and had coffee.

Soon Raymond looked up and said, "Alright people lets go and meet some Aliens." Everybody responded with enthusiasm, Wane and Cindy climb into the cockpit and began the preflight, Bonnie began to clear the cups and saucers.

The flight to the Cape would be very short they would stay under 10,000 feet. Given control tower permission, Wayne taxied out to the runway parked and ran the jets engines up. Cindy called control for permission to take off, it seemed they were no sooner in the air and Cindy called Cape Canaveral for permission to land, She identified the jet and they were given permission to land on the main north-south runway.

Wayne made a good one chirp landing and as soon as they slowed, a jeep appeared in front of them with a big 'Follow Me' sign on the back, they followed the jeep down to the main hanger and Wayne was shown where to park.

Wayne and Cindy were locking the Cessna down and Raymond and Bonnie climbed down the steps and walked over to the main hanger, with the Cessna locked, Wayne and Cindy followed them.

The reception committee continued to grow, there had not been enough time once everyone agreed it must be true and there were representatives from the White House, but no politicians. The head of The World Health Organization, and the head of NASA, the heads of space agencies that had managed to get there from around the planet were part of the welcoming committee.

Raymond spotted Eric Hoffman and started towards him with Bonnie following, Raymond shook hands with Eric and then Bonnie, "how are things going, we just got here." said Raymond.

Eric glanced at his watch, "they will be a little early, but everything is going fine, they have dropped their shield and they should be entering the atmosphere now, so we should be seeing them very shortly."

The public address system was on with speakers throughout the committee area, the Cape's air traffic control said the space ship was in the the atmosphere now and they would be crossing the west coast and flying across the lower states and the Gulf of Mexico and then they would turn final when they reached the Florida panhandle, everything was looking good, The welcoming committee was waiting in silent anticipation.

After another short wait, The public address system came on and said we have them on radar now, they have dropped their shield and they are slowing down, they are coming across the Florida panhandle and they will turn final at Jacksonville and follow the coast down here to the main north south runway.

Conversation began among the spectators as they commented and turned to gaze down the runway to the north and they waited, suddenly someone shouted, "there it is," they all turned to look north.

A dark line appeared above the end of the runway with two landing lights,

Neil was in manual control and he had the nose right on the center line, he touched down with a one chirp perfect landing and streaked pass the welcoming committee, If you had to describe the ship, it looked like a flying wing, like the US Navy's unmanned carrier aircraft, only much larger, it looked like the pictures of the US Air force's, long range stealth bombers.

The ship streaked pass the committee slowing down as it headed south, the jeep with the 'follow me' sign took off after them.

Neil at the controls slowed the ship and turned north as the jeep pulled in front of them, Neil was in contact with the Cape's air traffic control and he said, "we will have to wait forty-five minutes before we can open the hatches, we will have to become accustomed to the oxygen and atmosphere"

"Roger that, follow the jeep to the main hanger and park." said the control tower.

Neil followed the jeep and parked in front of the hanger and the welcome committee, They all studied the ship, a six foot human slightly stooped, could walk around under the ship, the landing gear dropped down from the body of the aircraft and the tires appeared to be made of rubber or something very similar.

Raymond moved over close to Mr. Hoffman, "It's very impressive isn't it?"

"Yes it is," said Mr. Hoffman as he turned to face Raymond. "I look at the bottom of that ship, look at the tires and I wonder why they didn't land that ship vertical, like a helicopter?"

"Neil is the pilot, the man you talked to, and as I said, he was here earlier and he landed and took off twice, he was in a much smaller ship, a reconnaissance ship, but he landed and took off vertically." Raymond explained.

"Mmm," said Mr. Hoffman as he stood contemplating the space ship.

"Looking at that ship, I guess they could have built it with Neil's planning and advice since he left here but I doubt it.., you know what this means," said Raymond, "It means there are other planets out there very similar to earth and advanced enough to have built runways."

"Right, yes, you are right, that is just what I was thinking," said Mr. Hoffman as he turned from looking at the ship and looked at Raymond, or they could use this ship for landing on their planet, well it will be interesting to talk about when they come out, he glanced at his watch, we have about 30 more minutes Bonnie and Cindy stood just behind the two men, they stood contemplating the space ship, waiting.

The head of the World Health Organization stood there with the heads of other space agencies from around the planet, the other committee members stood chatting as they waited.

Suddenly The murmurs of the crowd grew louder and stopped as a hatch on the bottom of the ship opened and stairwell steps moved down to the pavement, a member of the ships crew climbed down the steps, turned and watched the other five crew members climb down, they were dressed in silver flight suits, the first man was Neil, he turned and began to lead them towards the committee.

Suddenly Bonnie broke ranks and ran out to Neil in her high heels, she jumped into his arms and they kissed, Cindy began to clap, suddenly the whole committee joined in and began to applaud, after a moment the head of the World Health Organization spoke, "O.K. that's it, she goes right into quarantine with them," he turned and indicated to a man standing in a white coat with a white mask over his face, the man nodded and turned to lead the crew pass the committee into a large room with with a glass front. Bonnie and Neil still arm in arm turned back towards the glass.

Raymond managed to get to the glass ahead of the other committee members, Raymond spoke to Neil through the glass, "How are you, you are looking good," said Raymond.

"Fine, fine," said Neil, "it was a good landing."

"Yes it was," replied Raymond.

"Thats a fine looking ship.., who are all these other people you have here?"

Neil turned and looked back into the room.., "well let's see they are all from my planet and they are specialist in their fields, those two," he indicated two men who were talking across the room, "the man on your left, I guess on planet earth he would be a master engineer, his speciality is Mag-Lev High Speed Rail, you probably could not ask him a question he doesn't have an answer for and the man he is talking to is a physician, and over there, the one with his back to us is a biologist, the other one is an engineer specialization in electronics and nuclear physics. and the man next to him is a phycologist specializing in behavior.., they can speak some english but they are not all fluent."

"Well I'm sure that will not be a problem," said Raymond.

"Right," said Neil, "Huh, how long do you think they will keep us in here?"

"I don't know, It's the man from The World Health Organization, from the United Nations making the decisions." said Raymond.

"With the ship sitting out there.., the longer it sits and is seen from the air, the more rumors it will create." said Neil.

"Yes, I agree," said Raymond, "let me see if I can do something about that."

"It's locked but they can attach a tug to the front gear and pull it right in, said Neil.

"I talked to Mr. Hoffman about the ship and we were wondering why it's designed to make a standard landing, with a runway, your other ships made vertical landings, not all the planets you visit have runways," ask Raymond.

"No that ship is designed to land and take off from a runway, we use it mostly for landing on our home planet and the rare planets like planet earth that are advanced enough to have runways, it will carry a lot of cargo," said Neil.

Bonnie stood next to Neil, Raymond looked at her and said, "Bonnie are you going to be alright here, is there anything you need?" She moved over close to Neil and put her arm around his waist, "no, no, I'll be fine."

"Alright, I've been on the phone and I have got to go back to Houston, I'll take the Cessna Longitude and Cindy will probably have to go back to Jacksonville and wait at the office until we can find out how long the quarantine is going to last, when you get out, you will need transportation and Cindy can fly the Hawker Beechcraft back here, Neil do you have any specific plans, what you will do, where you will start?" ask Raymond.

"Yes, I believe The Mag-Lev High Speed rail will have to be built and the sooner the better, there is talk of building electric automobiles but it's talk that just seems to go on and on, they are building new fossil fuel burning automobiles every day and the old ones are still on the road filling the atmosphere with carbon monoxide and planet earth is going to have to pay for that and it may be a lot sooner then we think, Florida East Coast railroad has the right of way from Miami To Jacksonville and I think that is where we should start, we should have an office in Jacksonville and once we have a functioning Meg-Lev High Speed train running between Miami and Jacksonville, People will look at that and they will want it." Neil explained.

"Yes, I agree," said Raymond, "we have discussed that and then we come right back to the cost."

"Yes the cost will be there, but we have got to over come it and if we don't get started, planet earth is going to start dying from pulmonary disease," said Neil.

"I agree," said Raymond, "since we have been discussing this I have been looking at the automobile traffic and during rush hour, you can sit there bumper to bumper and look at the opposite lanes and there are head lights as far as you can see and you know, each of those cylinders

are combusting and pumping out carbon monoxide and the older the
vehicle is, the more carbon monoxide it is putting into the atmosphere
and you can smell it and as I fly around and look down, I can see the
trees being cut down that make the oxygen and you are right, I think the
time to get something done about this is growing shorter and shorter..,
O.K., let me find Hoffman and get that ship under cover and Bonnie you
have my personal number, I'll probably be in Houston but if you need
anything call me." With that said, Raymond turned in search of Mr.
Hoffman, he saw Cindy among the people standing around looking at
the glass, he took her by the arm and said, "Cindy we have got to get you
back to Jacksonville so you can wait at the office until we find out how
long this is going to take, he looked up and saw Mr. Hoffman talking
among other executives and he moved over with Cindy and stood there
waiting to get Mr. Hoffman's attention, Mr. Hoffman turned and saw
Raymond and Raymond began to explain what Neil said about the ship
needed to be put in the hanger, "Yes let me take care of that," said Mr.
Hoffman.

"He said the ship is locked but to just attach a tug to the front gear
and pull it in," Raymond added.

"Right, let me get some of our people," said Mr. Hoffman, as he
turned looking for some NASA engineers.

Raymond turned back to Cindy, "Cindy the head of The World
Health Organization is making the decisions on how long they will
have to be in quarantine.., I have got to get back to Houston, I want to
drop you off in Jacksonville and you can get with Bill Evans and make
sure the Hawker Beechcraft is ready to fly then go back to the office
and wait until The World Health Organization is ready to release these
people and then plan on flying down here and pick them up, are you
O.K. with that?"

"Yes, yes I can do that," said Cindy.

"O.K. come on," said Raymond as he turned for the Cessna, they
soon had the aircraft in sight and Wayne the pilot was waiting.

Raymond turned to Cindy, "can you file the flight plan for
Jacksonville and Houston?"

"Yes," answered Cindy.

"O.K., I'll get with Wayne and start the preflight," said Raymond.

With Wayne and Cindy in the cockpit and Raymond in the back with his cell phone, they had permission to take off on the main runway, as they taxied to position, they watched the space ship being pulled into the main hanger.

They were quickly on the ground in Jacksonville, Raymond took the copilots seat and told Cindy to get the Hawker Beechcraft ready and wait in the office for a phone call.

Cindy said O. K. as she climbed down out of the Cessna and stood and watched as Wayne taxied over to the main north south runway and took off for Houston.

Cindy got with Bill Evans and they pre-flighted the Hawker Beechcraft and made sure it was ready to go, Then Cindy took a cab back to the office and brought the secretary up to date, everybody settled down to wait.

Cindy was back at the office the next morning.

"Cindy, where are you?" Bonnie called Cindy on her cell.

"I'm back in Jacksonville at the office."

"Where is Mr. Crane?" Ask Bonnie.

"He had to go back to Houston," said Cindy, "I'm to wait here until you are free and then fly the Hawker down there."

"I've been trying to reach Mr. Crane, I can not with this phone and Neil's phone is locked up on the space ship, I have been talking to these guys and they have the supplies on the space ship and the knowledge to eliminate most of the disease on planet Earth including, Ebola, HIV-AIDS and Cancer, and they have told me it is a criminal offense to waste time on their planet, and it is a criminal offense to cut down a tree, almost the same as killing another person, they have the equipment and supplies to take care of anything that develops and they can not understand what the hold up is." said Bonnie.

"Mr. Crane is in the same position, he talked to Mr. Hoffman and Mr. Hoffman said it was up to The World Health Organization and The UN." said Cindy."

"Well I guess the UN is waiting to see if something happens, a transmission of some kind of disease or whatever, but the point is these people can handle just about anything that comes up and waiting is just a waste of time.

"Yes you are right, I think Mr. Crane went back to Houston because of a natural gas leak from one of the reservoirs.., some of these companies are pumping poison liquid into the ground water trying to get the natural gas out, and it poisons the animals and the people and now they have a leak from a major reservoir and it is leaking natural-gas, and this is a disaster for the planet," Cindy explained, "the leaking of methane gas into the atmosphere is worse then the automobiles and power stations burning fossil fuels."

"We have got to get that Meg-Lev built and we can not wait," said Bonnie, each day millions of automobiles are pumping carbon monoxide into the atmosphere and now we have methane gas you can not see boiling into the atmosphere and it is warming the planet and destroying the oxygen we must have and it is a terrible fire hazard."

"What do you think we can do?" Ask Cindy.

"I don't know, I just don't know," said Bonnie, "if you can reach Mr. Crane tell him I called, and if there is any way he can reach The World Health Organization and get them to break up this waiting, that will be the first answer to this impending disaster."

"All right, I'll call Mr. Crane and repeat what you just said and if you can get out of there, I'll bring the Beechcraft down for you and Neil, said Cindy.

Cindy hung up and then punched in Mr. Crane's cell number, Raymond answered immediately, "hello Mr. Crane, Cindy here, I just got a call from Bonnie, she has been trying to reach you and for some reason, her cell phone can not reach you," Cindy then repeated what Bonnie said.., "Yes, I know, we have a major gas leak over here," said Raymond, "and I agree we have an impending disaster.., "Huh, let me call Mr. Hoffman over at NASA he knows the head of The World Health organization and if anybody can convince him it should be Mr. Hoffman."

Raymond punched in Mr. Hoffman's number, his secretary came on the phone, Raymond explained who he was and Mr. Hoffman picked up the phone, "Hello, good afternoon, Mr. Hoffman," said Raymond, "I just got off the phone with one of our people, they still have Bonnie and the aliens from the space ship locked up over at Cape Canaveral, Bonnie has been communicating with them and she says on their planet it is a crime to cut down a tree, it is a severe criminal act, equivalent to murder, and wasting time is also a crime and they have the knowledge and drugs locked up on the space ship that will cure Ebola, HIV-AIDS and Cancer and they are sure that if they brought anything here from outer space that could contaminate planet Earth, they can handle it.., and they can not understand why they are wasting time.., now with that said, I have a potential disaster on my hands here, I have a natural gas leak and this one is the equivalent of about 4.5 million vehicles running up and down the highways each day and this is not the only leak we have, there are leaks all over the country, this new fracking technology is good in that natural gas burns cleaner then fossil fuels but fracking has expanded the area being drilled and the wear and tear on the natural gas system and equipment has created a lot of dangerous situations, dangerous situations for this planet, I need the help of the people from the space ship, I call them people because I don't like calling them aliens, in short Mr. Hoffman how can I get those people free so they can help us?"

"Well I can see your point, but The World Health Organization, when they heard the space ship was coming in here they immediately took interest but there was no proof and when they got proof the ship was actually coming in, they took over, that is the UN and the World Health Organization, it has all happened so fast nobody was prepared, and now the UN is in charge or they have taken charge.., huh, let me see if I can talk to the man over at the The World Health Organization and see if we can do something about canceling the quarantine."

"Make the point that it would help a lot of people that are trying to avoid a major catastrophe for planet earth." said Raymond Crane.

"I will," said Mr. Hoffman as he hung up.

It was some time later Raymond received a phone call from Mr. Hoffman,

"They took this all the way to the top at the UN and they decided to make one more examination and if everyone passed, they would lift the quarantine, it should happen sometime this afternoon." Mr Hoffman explained.

"Well that certainly is good news," said Raymond, "I hoping one of the engineers will know how to stop this gas leak or be able to show us how."

"Lets hope so," said Mr. Hoffman.

"O K, I can not get there in time from here so I am going to send a Hawker Beechcraft down from Jacksonville to pick up Bonnie and Neil, can they get clearance to land at the Cape?"

"I'll make sure, it's a Hawker Beechcraft jet you say?"

"Yes Cindy is the pilot and I'm sure she will file a flight plan so they will know she is coming." said Raymond.

"Alright good, well you keep me posted on that gas leak and I will take care of things here, said Mr. Hoffman.

"I will and I appreciate the effort, said Raymond as he hung up.

Raymond called Cindy in Jacksonville and filled her in on what he had discussed with Mr. Hoffman, "you can Take Bill Evans as copilot, I'm not sure if he is qualified with the Hawker Beechcraft so you can call it a training flight.

"O K, will do, you say the Beechcraft is cleared to land at the Cape?" said Cindy.

"Yes it will be and tell Bonnie to call me as soon as she is out." said Raymond as he hung up.

Cindy got into a cab and headed for the Airport, she found Bill Evans and began to fill him in, "What?" you say they are Aliens.., Aliens from outer space?" Bill was in oil stained coveralls, "alright let me change, you file a flight plan we'll pull the Beechcraft out and be on our way."

Cindy returned with the flight plan and they attached the tug to the Beech Craft, Cindy said, "I forget to ask, are you qualified with the Beechcraft?"

"I have a few hours but I am not fully qualified," said Bill.

"O.K., I filed as a training flight," Cindy answered. They pulled the Hawker out onto the ramp and pointed it so the exhaust would not interfere with other people or aircraft and climbed aboard, Cindy fired both engines and pulled over to the waiting area for the north south runway and waited for permission to take off. They were in the air for a short period and Cindy ask Bill to call the cape for permission to land.

They landed and followed the 'follow me' jeep to the main hanger and parked, they climbed out of the Hawker Beechcraft and were walking towards the main hanger, "this is where the space ship is locked down, it looks just like it belongs here on earth, it looks like the Navy's

UAV, the ones they fly off carriers only much bigger and it looks like pictures of The Air force's long range stealth bombers, when the shield is up, nobody can see it, that's why so few people know they are here, nobody believed it until they were ready to touch down here at the Cape and they dropped the shield." Cindy explained.., they walked over to the hanger and peered in.

"Will you look at that, you are right it does look like it belongs here," said Bill.

"Let's go see if we can find Bonnie and the crew." said Cindy.

They turned for the quarantine part of the hanger and the glass partition, Bonnie was there with Neil, "you never met Neil did you?" Cindy asked, "that's him with Bonnie, everybody in this room is an Alien and part of the ship's crew except Bonnie."

"You sure would never guess that," said Bill, "they look like everybody else around here."

Bonnie was sitting on a couch with Neil, she looked up saw Cindy and jumped to her feet rushing over, "Cindy you are here!"

"Yes we got word that you would have one more examination and if everyone passed they would end the quarantine this afternoon, Bill and I brought the Hawker Beechcraft down."

"Oh that's great, we heard rumors but no one would confirm it."

"Have you had an examination recently?" ask Cindy.

"Yes we just finished," said Bonnie.

"Good well maybe they are about to open the door," said Cindy.

"How did you get word?" Ask Bonnie.

"Mr. Crane, he has a major gas leak over in east Texas, he didn't have time to get here after he heard they would be ending the quarantine so he called me, he really wants to talk to Neil."

Suddenly the door in the back of the room opened and several men entered the room, Bonnie turned as Cindy looked up, "oh it's the Doctor," said Bonnie, she walked over and joined Neil in listening to what was being said. After a few minutes Bonnie took Neil's arm and led him over to Cindy on the other side of the glass, "It's over," said Bonnie, "they are going to lift the quarantine, we are free to go." She turned to Neil, "Neil this is Cindy and this is Bill Evans, he is head of aviation for

Crane Industries in Jacksonville," the two men could not shake hands through the glass and they nodded and made a slight bow at each other.

"Mr. Crane is very anxious to see you," Cindy said looking at Neil, "he has a major gas leak over in East Texas, he didn't have time to come here after he heard they may lift the quarantine so he sent me down here from Jacksonville with the Hawker Beechcraft, can you come?"

"Well I guess so," said Neil, "let me check with the other crew 'members and find out what their plans are now that we have been released," Neil touched Bonnie's arm and turned for the group of men. "Bonnie turned for the door, "is the door unlocked can we get out?" Bonnie ask as she turned for the door, the three of them moved over to the door and opened it, Bonnie was free.

"We topped off the tanks on the Hawker Beechcraft when we left Jacksonville," said Cindy, "so if Neil can come we are ready to go to East Texas."

"Here comes Neil now," said Bonnie

Neil was grinning as he approached them, he had a cell phone in his hand and he showed it to them, "the top man from the UN gave me this and said to stay in touch, he knows about the gas leak and he wants me to go out and take a look, the rest of the crew are going to fly to the UN in New York and I am going to report to him after I take a look at the leak."

"OK, I guess we are ready to fly then," said Bonnie.

Cindy filed a training flight plan to Houston and the four of them climbed into the Hawker Beechcraft, they would need fuel before they got to Houston and Cindy and Bill had missed lunch, they decided to land at Biloxi Mississippi, top off the fuel and Bill went for a couple of sandwiches, Bonnie and Neil were content with coffee.

They took off from Biloxi and the FAA diverted them around an area on the Gulf Coast north of Houston, it's where the gas was leaking.

Cindy flew to Houston and landed at the airfield, she taxied over to the Crane Industries hanger and parked, it was almost sunset, she shut down the engines and Neil opened the door and looked up and saw Raymond Crane walking towards them from the hanger, he had his hand out as he approached Neil, "Neil how are you?"

"Fine, fine, how are you?" "You are looking good," answered Neil.

"Thank you, I want to apologize for the UN World Health Organization putting you in quarantine, when we got word you were coming, the WHO was interested but with your shield up nobody could see you and there was a lot of skepticism that you were really there, The UN was interested and they were skeptic, but they were the first at the Cape and they just took over."

"It's O.K. no real harm done, except wasted time, how is your problem with the gas leak?" Said Neil.

"It's a problem alright we need time to talk about it in the morning after you get a good nights rest." said Raymond."

Raymond looked past Neil and said, "Ladies, how are you, Bonnie and Cindy, Bill you doing alright?"

Everyone smiled and agreed they were O.K., Raymond looked down at Bonnie's feet, "Bonnie do you have more comfortable shoes?" "We are going to have to do some walking in the morning."

"Yes, I have some in my luggage," answered Bonnie.

"Are those good for walking?" He ask Cindy.

She had on high running shoes to be comfortable while flying, "Yes they will be fine," answered Cindy.

Raymond turned to Bill, "Bill go inside and find Wayne, he's working on the Cessna, I know you will want to talk with him, and then would you get the Hawker ready to fly, there is a reservation at the hotel for you, I am going to take Neil and these ladies out to the gas leak in the morning and the Hawker will probably be flying after that."

"Yes sir," said Bill with a slight bow and then he turned for the hanger.

Raymond turned back to the others, "We will take an automobile out to the leak, we can get within about a mile of it and then we will have to walk in, they have evacuated the area and police are posted all around to keep the curious out, my secretary has made reservations at the hotel so we can all get an early start in the morning."

They took the luggage out of the Jet and turned to walk around the Hanger, Raymond had a Mercedes parked there. "Bonnie you have a valid driver's license, why don't you drive," said Raymond, "I have got to go back into the hanger, you have hotel reservations at the hotel so just park in the garage and check into the hotel, we will meet in the morning at eight and drive up to the gas leak."

Bonnie drove to the company garage, her and Neil in the front and Cindy in the back, they left the automobile in the garage and walked over to the hotel and checked in, there were four rooms reserved but only three were used, Bonnie and Neil did not yet have a chance to get intimate since Neil left for the mother ship and they were anxious to make up for lost time, they agreed to meet for dinner in an hour.

After an hour Cindy found a comfortable chair in the lobby facing the elevator, soon she looked up and saw the elevator door open and Neil and Bonnie walked out, they looked up saw Cindy and walked over smiling, "have you heard from Bill yet?" Ask Bonnie.

"No," answered Cindy.

"Lets check with the desk and see if he has checked in," said Bonnie.

"No, there is still one room reserved for Crane Industries but no one by that name has checked in." said the desk clerk. "Any messages for Crane Industries," ask Bonnie.

"No, no it's pretty quite," said the clerk.

"O.K. thanks," said Bonnie as she reached into her purse for her cell phone, she punched in the number for the airport and ask for Bill. "hold on he's over with Ted Bishop," said the voice on the phone. Bill's voice was quickly on the phone, "no it's O.K., I'll have dinner with Ted Bishop and then I'll check into the hotel if it's all right I'll see you in the morning."

"Mr. Crane is going to pick us up at eight o'clock in the morning and take us out to the gas leak." said Bonnie.

"O.K., I'll have plenty to do here until you get back." said Bill.

"Good," said Bonnie, "I think we will be flying tomorrow."

"I should be ready." said Bill.

Bonnie clicked off, put the cell in her purse and looked up. "O.K., what are you in the mood for?" She ask.

"We can eat here or walk back to the garage get the car and find a another place," said Cindy. "I don't know what we are in for tomorrow, but I vote we eat here and get a good nights sleep."

"Sounds good to me," said Bonnie, as she turned to look at Neil, He nodded yes smiling, they walked into the dinning room sat down and ordered from the menu. Neil began to ask questions, bringing himself up to date on events that happened while he was away returning to the space ship. Bonnie and Cindy told him about the lectures on High Speed rail and the Mag-Lev rail system, she commented on how enthusiastic they all became when she talked of Mag-Lev with no pollution and little maintenance and then she said she did not tell them about the cost, She knew it was going to be high but she didn't know how high.

"It's going to be high alright," said Neil, "but not as high as the cost are going to be if they don't do something about this pollution."

"I agree," said Cindy, "the cost my be high, but once they get it in they will have something they can treasure for generations."

"So how long has this gas leak been going on?" Ask Neil.

"It just started," said Bonnie, "Mr. Crane left the Cape after you arrived, to look into it."

"Mmm, well I guess there is not much point in discussing it until we get up there and take a look," said Neil.

"Cindy how do you like that Hawker Beechcraft?" Neil ask.

"I like it, it's a real sweet aircraft, it's very appealing to look at when it's parked and it flies well."

They continued to finish the dinner and Neil spoke, "well ladies I guess we had better go and get that good nights sleep and If Mr. Crane is going to be here at eight we had better leave a wake up call for 6 O'clock, so we can have breakfast."

On the way upstairs they stopped at the front desk, left a wake up call and then Cindy went to her room and Neil and Bonnie went to the same room.

Bonnie had her bag in the room, Neil said, "give me a minute," as he turned for the bath, "wait," said Bonnie, she walked over and reached into her bag and handed him a toothbrush and a tube of toothpaste, "I picked this up earlier," she said. Neil accepted it with a smile and turned for the bath.

After a few minutes Neil came out, he had his shirt and trousers folded on his arm and he had a towel wrapped around his body, Bonnie was partially undressed, wait just a minute," she said as she turned for the bath, Neil was busy with turning the bed back and he sat in the chair with the towel still wrapped around him when Bonnie came out with a towel wrapped around her, he looked up, "let me look at that beautiful body," he said. She let the towel go at the top and opened it with both hands, "there you are," she said.

Neil left his towel in the chair, stood, took her in his arms and pressed their bare flesh together as they embraced an kissed. Neil bent over and started to put his arms under her knees and stopped, "whoa, it's a little early for that," he said, "I'll have to wait for at least 30 days," he led her over to the bed, they embraced and Bonnie lay on the bed and Neil climbed on with her, they embraced again....

Bonnie lay with her head on his chest, they talked, "when I got back to headquarter's the physicians had been working on a new medication that would help crews adapt to gravity on new planets, they gave me some, it's in the form of a pill and it has to be taken each day for thirty days, after which you should be adapted to that planet.., don't let me forget to take it."

The wake up call came on time and they woke, dressed and went down to the lobby, very shortly Cindy stepped off the elevator.

"We can go over and have breakfast at the company cafeteria, but I am not sure when they open, do you want so see if the hotel's open?" said Bonnie. "yes let's try here," said Cindy, Neil agreed as they turned for the hotel restaurant.

The restaurant had just opened and the staff were busy getting ready for the breakfast crowd, They picked a table and a waiter brought over menu's and left them to chose while he prepared the table, he was soon back with water and he stood with pad and pen, Neil looked up, "Ladies," he said, Bonnie and Cindy looked up, "O.K., I'll take..., said Bonnie and the orders were given and the three sat waiting.

"How does the food here compare with food in space and on your mother ship?" Cindy ask.

"The food here is wonderful, the variety and amount, the big problem is to watch how much you eat and be careful you don't quickly become over weight and join the other overweights you see waddling down the street." said Neil.

"Yes I can see that would be a problem," said Cindy.

They continue to finish the breakfast and Bonnie was looking at the check when her cell phone rang, she reached into her purse and brought out the cell phone, "Hello, Oh hello, good morning, yes we are just finishing breakfast," she listening to the phone in silence, "yes we will be out front."

She looked up, "You can probably guess, that was Mr. Crane, he is on his way in a limousine, he will be here in about twenty minutes, he will park out front, so we need to be ready, if anybody needs to go back upstairs, we better hurry along, I'll take care of this," she sat looking down at the check.

Cindy stood and took off for the elevator.

Neil stood waiting for Bonnie and they both started for the elevator.

In about twenty minutes the three of them stood on the curb as Mr. Crane's company limousine pulled up, Raymond motioned for them to get in, the limousine had a seat across the back and two seats facing the rear, there was a glass partition between the passenger section and the driver, it was a very good place to have a conversation.

Everyone settled down, Cindy was on the back seat opposite Raymond and Bonnie and Neil sat in the two seats facing the back, Raymond pushed a button and said, "O.K. Frank." The engine started and the limousine pulled away from the curb heading North, Raymond looked up, "It's o.k., he was up there yesterday, he knows where to go and how to get there.., I see everybody is prepared to go," he said, as he looks at the shoes everyone is wearing, "we can drive to about a mile from the leak and then we have to walk, the last quarter mile is kinda rough."

"Just what's going on up there? I got a briefing but they really didn't know much," said Neil.

"Well lets see," said Raymond, "It's called 'FRACKING' they have found they can pump a new liquid into the ground where there is natural gas, and get the gas out which is a good thing because natural gas burns cleaner then fossil fuels, the problem is the liquid they pump into the ground poisons the ground water and the animals that try to drink it die and it is poisoning human beings, now in addition to that there has been a lot of profit made selling the gas and in making the profit the land owners and the people pumping the gas out have not reinvested in the drilling equipment, the original pipes and equipment are old and they come in with new equipment and start drilling and the old pipes break and start leaking and that is what we have here, the original pipe was pumping from a gas dome and the pipe broke some ways down and started leaking gas, it is leaking carbon monoxide into the atmosphere at the rate or equivalent of 4.5 million vehicles running up and down the highways each day and the people who own the land and the people who are making a profit producing power don't want to hear about how they are polluting the atmosphere."

"Yes I know, I know, I was telling Bonnie earlier about how the almost same thing happened on my planet, they were producing power and pumping carbon monoxide into the atmosphere until people started to die from pulmonary disease, the dying grew into the hundreds and then into the hundreds of thousands and the people producing the power suddenly looked up and realized they had to do something, now if you think producing a Mag-Lev high speed rail system and cutting back on the production of carbon monoxide producing vehicles is expensive, look at the cost of cutting back on power production and pumping oxygen back into the atmosphere." Neil explained.

"I know," said Raymond, "I was driving back to Houston and I looked up and saw smoke billowing into the air, I thought someone's house or building was burning down, I drove over there and saw a man out in a field, he was cutting down the trees on the property, piling them up, throwing gasoline on them and burning them, instead of using trucks and cutting equipment to clear the land, he was just cutting them down and burning them. I ask him if he knew he was cutting down the trees that were producing the oxygen we needed to breath on this planet plus he was filling the atmosphere with tons of smoke and ash."

He looked at me and said, "I own this land and I can do anything I want to with it."

"That stopped me, he was right, he had the attitude the colonist from Europe had who came over to this virgin land in the 1600's, the problem is, this is not the 17th century, this is the twenty first century and we can not act and we can not live the way they did in the 1600's. this attitude of, I want to plant more crops so I'll just cut those trees down and plant there, that kind of thinking would work in the 1600's, they did not have anything else polluting the atmosphere but now we have got to overcome that attitude and change the way we live." explained Raymond.

There was a pause of silence as everyone sat thinking, "that's what we are up against sure enough," commented Raymond.., "the problem is when you have a man making a profit and it is legal, it is very difficult to get him to stop and take the risk of changing to something else."

"That's true," said Bonnie, "and it dose not matter if the change will help this whole planet, some people just will not listen."

There was more silence and Raymond looked up and said, "O.K. we are getting close, we will have to get through a police line, that's why I brought the limo, it should give us some authority but make sure you do not have cigarettes, lighters or matches, that is what the police will be looking for, anything with a spark could blow the whole thing."

There were vehicles parked in a line, the driver drove the limo up front where the police were, a policeman came out and motioned for the driver to park over to the side, everyone began to climb out of the limo and a police officer who looked to be in charge came over and acknowledged Raymond.

"Hello Sargent,"said Raymond, "I've told everyone not to carry anything that could make a spark, You might remind them once more."

The police officer nodded he understood and said, "O.K. folks make sure you do not have anything that could cause a spark, matches, lighters.., one spark could ignite all the gas here." Everyone nodded in agreement.

Raymond turned and looked to make sure everyone was ready, "O.K. people it's just over that rise there, about a quarter of a mile, you will be able to see the tops of he drills when we get up there," they started walking, Cindy was bringing up the rear, "Pray nobody strikes a match." she said.

THE END

THE SPY

Cast of characters

NEIL Conrad ------------------------------- visiting Alien
Bonnie Stewart ---------------------------- Head of Public Relations
Raymond Crane --------------------------- Head of Crane Industries
Cindy Collins ------------------------------ Pilot Crane Industries, Asst.
PR Erick Hoffman ------------------------- Head of NASA
Wayne Edwards --------------------------- Head of Crane Ind. aviation
Ben Hadley -------------------------------- Head of Advertising
Bill Evans --------------------------------- Head of aviation Jacksonville

High Water

A
Novella
by
Paul T White

I<small>T WAS LATE WINTER NOW</small> but here where he was, it was Spring and up north snow was still on the ground. The strange part of it was here where he walked, all around him looked like a very large category 5 hurricane had just passed through and yet it was well past hurricane season.

Small houses that had been water front on the ocean were now off their foundations and scattered along the highway. Automobiles, were upturned everywhere. The only buildings that remained were the high-rise concrete structures but the bottom floors all showed damage.

He had been in south Florida when he first heard the news reports, a large meteor was heading for earth and due to impact and there was not much that could be done about it with todays technology.

He started late in the day and had driven north, keeping his ear close to the car radio. The latest predictions were, there would be an impact on the eastern seaboard of the United States. The defense department could do nothing but warn everybody and try to get them prepared .

His home was in north Florida and he was trying to get back there, he had driven into the night and finally at Daytona Beach he stopped at a high-rise motel on the highest ground he could find. He had them give him a room on the fifth floor, he did not want to get too high.

He lay in the bed dozing, waking periodically to listen to the radio bulletins and then the latest bulletin, the impact area would be the

Atlantic ocean north of Puerto Rico, he knew this was the deepest part of the Atlantic ocean.

The motel management called and said they were evacuating the beach, he did not have to go but he was advised to.

Part of him wanted to go but a larger part of him wanted to stay. He stood at the window gazing to the east southeast where the impact was expected, he decided he was almost home now and there was not much he could do out on the highway, he was comfortable here, he lay back on the bed and waited.

He could have remained sleeping because when the meteor impacted the atmosphere there was a large sonic boom, all the windows on the east side were cracked or broken and the impact in the ocean some 500 miles to the east southeast finished off the windows.

He stood at the window, the sun was just breaking the horizon when the first and largest Tsunami came in, he stood and watched as a dark line appeared on the ocean, he watched it grow and grow as it came in, he stood and watched the water swirl under him at the bottom of the motel, he stood there and watched until the last of the smaller waves dissipated and then he climbed down the steps to the lobby, the second floor was damaged and the ground floor and lobby were completely destroyed, he walked through what was left of the lobby to the entrance to the parking lot. he looked about him, the landscape had completely changed, everything that could move was moved by the water, the telephone and light poles were still there and the high-rise buildings still stood but the sand dunes around them were changed by the water, overturned automobiles were scattered everywhere, he searched and searched for his automobile and finally gave up and concluded it was at the bottom of the Halifax river, the (ICW), the Inter coastal Waterway, that ran through Daytona Beach and separated the town.

When the first alerts came in the authorities tried to get everybody off the beach and now that most were off, the bridges were closed and nobody could get back on.

He stood there gazing about him and suddenly he reached into his pocket and pulled out his cell phone, he pressed it on and then pressed 911 and miracle of miracles he got an operator over at the airport, he identified himself and said he wanted to report his automobile missing for insurance purposes, suddenly another voice came on the phone.., the voice ask who he was, where he was and what he could see?

He stood with the phone to his ear slowly turning one way then the other and then he began to speak.., "It looks like a very large hurricane has passed through, everything that could move has moved but the strange thing is the palm trees and other trees where their foundation and roots were not washed away are still standing, their leaves still intact as if nothing happened but there are overturned automobiles everywhere, store fronts are smashed in, sand dunes, where they could be are washed onto and across the highway, houses that were ocean front have been carried up on the highway and smashed as the water moved them..," he paused a moment not speaking.

The voice on the other end of the line spoke, "are you alright?"

"Yes, I'm fine except for my automobile, I would like to report it missing for insurance purposes and then I am going to start north."

The voice on the cell phone answered, "alright what is your name?"

The man standing holding the phone to his ear said; "My name is Frank Cooper, I am from north of here and I want to get back and see if I still have a house."

"Alright," came the voice on the cell, "Mr. Cooper we have your name and a recording of this conversation, that should suffice for insurance purposes, we have your cell phone number, what is your address.., can you describe the automobile?"

"I have a house in the Greenwood area of Jacksonville, my automobile is a two year old Ford Mustang," he continued to describe the automobile and paused.

"Mr. Cooper we are going to keep the bridges closed for a while, you may have a problem with transportation."

"It's O.K., I'm going to start walking north on A1A, hopefully I will be able to catch a ride farther on."

"Alright we have a record of this conversation and later if we find your automobile we will contact you."

"O.K. fine, Thank You."

"Alright this 911 line will stay open, Good Luck," said the voice on the other end of the line.

"Thank You," he repeated and pressed the phone off.

Frank Cooper turned and started walking north, He had his luggage in his left hand and he could see where the sand dunes where open to the ocean, the water pushed the sand up onto AIA, blocking the street and he had to walk around it, he continued to walk, occasionally he came upon another human being who in a dazed state was out surveying their property or what was left of it, they seemed to dazed to acknowledge him and he continued to walk.

He walked on into the morning and came to a large shopping center built off AIA with a large parking lot between the front door and the street or highway, a 35 or 40 foot sport fishing boat sat on it's keel tilted slightly to starboard. It sat in front of a WAL-Mart store and it looked so strange with automobiles laying on their sides washed up against the building, the boat looked like it was put their for advertising purposes, it's outriggers were still up.

He continued to walk into the morning and was coming to the end of Daytona Beach, the buildings were spaced out and the sand dunes had low scrub vegetation and palmetto covering it and where the vegetation grew the sand was still in tact. He came upon the partial roof of a green and white bungalow laying in the middle of the street, the gabled end faced him with the rectangle vent still in tact and shingles still attached to what was left of the roof, he walked around the debris and spotted an automobile sitting upright on all four wheels, it seemed so strange as if it was parked there, he continued on and as he came near the automobile he saw that it was parked there and on the other side he saw a figure bent over searching in the debris that was left of the foundation of a house. He walked around the end of the automobile and approached the figure, the figure sensed him and stood facing him, he saw it was a woman, middle aged, about his age, she wore jeans and a long sleeved cotton top, the jeans were tight and they displayed a very nice figure for a woman of her age.

"Hello," he spoke to the woman as she turned towards him.

"Hello," the woman answered.

"I would say, good morning but it doesn't look to good," said Frank, is this your house?"

"Yes.., it was," said the woman.

"Well it can be rebuilt, was anyone hurt?" he ask.

"No it's just me," said the woman as she began to relax after hearing him speak, "luckily I have all my papers, title, insurance, etc, in a safety deposit box at the bank," added the woman.

Frank coming closer saw she was a very attractive woman with blond hair tied in a bun in back.

"My name is Frank Cooper," he said, "I think I have a house in the southern suburbs of Jacksonville, I was in south Florida when I first heard the news about the meteor, it was predicted to impact the eastern seaboard, I started driving back and stopped at the Balmoral motel south of here."

"That was a good choice," said the woman, "My name is Ester."

"That's a pretty name Ester, it's not used very often,"

"Thank you," said Ester, "I have always liked it."

He nodded smiling at her an then he continued, "I saw the Balmoral was on the highest ground along there and it wasn't until I checked in that the news came on the radio that the impact would be in the ocean north of Porto Rico, I decided to stay where I was, luckily I had the blinds closed when the sonic boom hit, it broke all the glass on the east side of the motel, I stood and watched the first wave come in, it was the biggest and with my layman's observation it was fifty feet when it crested, after that all the waves coming in were smaller." He paused for a moment.

"I waited in the motel until the water settled back into the ocean and then I climbed down the stairs, the second floor was damaged and the ground floor including the lobby was just washed away, I walked out into the parking lot and it too was just washed clean, I began a search for my car, I looked everywhere and finally gave up and tried 911 on my cell, i got right through, they are located over at the airport, I told them I wanted to report my automobile missing and a voice came on the phone wanting to know who I was and what I could see, I spent about five minutes describing what I could see and he concluded by saying they where closing all the bridges and letting no one back on the beach, I told him I was going to start walking north."

Ester stood there giving him her full attention, finally after he paused, sheturned and looked at the trail of debris that had been her house and said, "well I guess I may as well bid that farewell," then she turned as if to walk to her car.

"Wait," said Frank, "do you have a camera?"

Ester just looked at him and shook her head.

Frank set his bag down and reached into his pocket and pulled out his cell phone, he began to click photos of the foundation then he ask her to stand where the door had been and he got a couple of shots of her with the bare foundation in the background, he turned and began to take shots of the debris trail leading down to the gabled end of the roof now blocking A1A, a red lifeguard's chair or stand was in the background laying on it's back it's feet or bottom of the stand pointing to the west.

Ester stood back, a little relieved now to let someone else make the decisions.

Frank, finished and turned to her, "It doesn't matter how good your insurance company is, the more evidence you can produce showing the loss, the easier and quicker the claim will be settled," he said.

Ester nodded and said, "yes, I understand."

Frank paused and said, "what are you going to do now?"

"I don't know, said Ester, "when they announced to get off the beach last night, I just grabbed a bag and jumped into the car, I drove up to the rest stop on I-95 and slept in the car, I came back at first light and crossed a bridge north of here, I guess I got there before they closed it off.., I have relations in Kentucky and Ohio, I guess I'll go up there," she paused not sure what more to say.

Frank walked over next to her, opened the cell phone and began to scroll the photo's he had taken, Ester stood studying them.

"We can find out where to send them, the claims department of the insurance company, and we can just send them over electronically, Ester turned, looked at him and smiled. Frank clicked the camera off, turned and looked around him, "well I guess there is no reason to hang around here..," he turned to Ester and said, "I would like to get a ride up to Duval county and see if I still have a house.."

"Sure," said Ester as she turned for the car, "come on."

They drove up A1A avoiding the debris and sand that had washed up on the highway.

Ester began to speak, "my husband and I came down from Ohio and bought that house, I really loved that place and living close to the sea.., my husband never did take to it, I think it made him nervous living that close to the water, he never did say so but I think it did and then one thing led to the next and we divorced, he gave me the house and moved back up to Ohio, I was getting regular letters from him but I haven't heard from him in a while, I think he may have met someone else.., I think he was just glad to get away."

Ester drove keeping her eyes on the road and glancing over at Frank occasionally as she spoke, "the bridge I came over on is just ahead, I think I will cross back over."

"That sounds good, I am sure we will make better time," said Frank.

There was no traffic and they did not see other people, Ester had to concentrate on the road as she drove, they left Daytona Beach and the houses and buildings were sparsely built here along the beach, the dunes were higher, almost a bluff but the water still came up and washed over to the ICW and dissipated, the low growth, palmetto and other vegetation held the sand.

They began to see high-rises or multiple storied buildings and then a small cluster of buildings, Frank was not sure if it qualified as a town, "up here I'll turn left and go back over the ICW," said Ester as she concentrated on the road.

As they crested the top of the bridge and looked down they could see a strobe light flashing on the top of a police cruiser, Ester slowed as she approached the cruisers, several police officers stood about, one walked to the center of the road holding up his hand, Ester came to a stop next to the officer.

Ester identified herself and said she had driven back onto the beach to check on her house and it was completely gone, another officer with sergeant strips stood at Frank's window, Frank and Ester began to relate where they had been and what they had seen, finally Frank and Ester in telling their stories concluded by saying they did not think there were many people on the beach, there were some but not many. The sergeant finally said they were about to send a patrol car over but the beach would be closed a while longer. Ester and Frank drove on.

Remarkably here on the west side of the ICW everything looked undisturbed, Frank pointed out how it looked as if nothing happened.

Ester looked over and said, "we are approaching U.S.1 and did he think they should take it?"

"We can probably make better time on U.S. 95," said Frank.

Ester continued on.

As they approached I-95, they could see it was as busy as normal, traffic flowing north and south, Ester took the right entrance lane onto i95 and joined the traffic flowing north, after a while she looked over at Frank and said, "the rest stop where I spent the night is right up here, do you want to stop?"

"Yeah let's make a pit stop and I would like to talk to some people and see what the thinking is," said Frank raising his voice over the noise or the car's movement.

Ester pulled into the parking lot and found a parking spot in the shade of a tree, they locked the car and went inside and parted heading for the rest rooms.

Frank began to chat with the men as he went about his business, he finished and came out looking for Ester, he spotted her over by the souvenir counter, she was talking to a woman, she spotted Frank, excused herself and joined Frank, they slowly walked back to the car."

"They seem totally unaware," Frank began, "they are aware a meteor hit the ocean but they are unaware of a tsunami hitting the beach, I mentioned the damage and to stall off any invasion of sightseers I told them the beach was blocked off by he police.

They returned to the car and sat with the windows open so they could talk without the noise of the car's movement.

"I lost my wife several years ago to cancer and since that time I have been trying to adjust to the bachelors life or living alone, it takes some getting used to," Frank begins to speak.

"Yes, I know what you mean," said Ester.

"I love the sea too and I have always lived near it," continued Frank, the house I have now is on a lake and I bought it because it was such a good deal, after my wife died I had a little cash and I found this place and it was just irresistible but there is a lot of room for just one person."

There was a pause in the conversation and Ester spoke, "well I guess we may as well get started and see if your house still stands. "Yes you are right," said Frank as he raised the window on his side, the temperature was not that hot but the window closed made the ride more comfortable.

They continued up I-95, Jacksonville was a major city and it too was separated by a river that ran through the center of the city, the river was the St. Johns river, the St. Johns was created and fed by fresh water springs south of the city and it like a few other rivers on the continent flowed north. Jacksonville had many bridges and the center of the city was located some twenty miles from the ocean where the river emptied into the sea. A tsunami would have little effect this far inland except to raise the water on the banks of the river.

Jacksonville's suburbs reached all the way down to the county line to the south and Frank's house was on a lake in one of the southern suburbs.

Ester continued to drive as they tried to get news on the radio.

St. Augustine is the first city south of Jacksonville, it has an inlet where the ICW empties into the sea. I-95 is about seven miles to the west of the city, they continue on not taking the time to investigate.

"St. Augustine will have suffered a lot of damage" said Frank, "you can look out from the center of the city and see the sea buoy marking the channel, the ICW runs through the center of town and the only thing protecting them from the sea is a very thin barrier island," Frank paused then added, "I can just see that wave cresting and washing over the barrier island then flooding the city.., there will be a lot of beach houses washed away." Ester glanced over at him then put her eyes back on the road and continued to drive, "there is nothing we can do but stay out of the way," she said.

"Yes, you are right they will not need a bunch of sightseers in the way." added Frank.

They continued on in silence and after some miles, Frank broke the silence, "we are getting close to the turn off, here it is up here, take the off ramp for state road 14, then turn right."

Ester followed his instructions, she put the indicator on and began slowing for the off ramp, she waited at the bottom of the off ramp for the traffic to thin and then pulled onto state road 14.

"There is a traffic light down about two blocks," said Frank, "you will want to turn left."

After the turn at the light, Frank looking about him began to comment, "well from the looks of things here you would never know anything happened on the beach, things here could not be more normal," he was silent and then added, my subdivision is about 1/2 a mile up here on the right."

Ester pulled into a gated community and stopped at the gate, a guard came out, Ester had her window down.

"Hello Fred," said Frank from the passenger side

The guard bent over peering into the automobile, "Oh hello Mr. Cooper, I didn't recognize the car."

"It belongs to the lady, she is giving me a ride," said Frank.

"Did you feel any effect from the meteor?" continued Frank.

"No it's all over the news.., they say there was a sonic boom but I slept right through it," answered Fred.

"No damage around here?" ask Frank.

"No, no, everything's quiet around here," said Fred.

"O.K., we are going to drive down to the house," said Frank, "you have a good day."

"O.K., Mr. Cooper, thank you, you have a good day."

Ester following Frank's directions drove into the complex, she saw she was in an upper middle class neighborhood, the street was lined with shade trees and driveways that led up to houses in the 300 to 600 thousand plus price range, "here the next driveway on the right," said Frank, "just drive up to the garage."

Ester pulled up to the garage and turned to Frank.

"I've been gone about three days," said Frank, "unless I've had a burglary,

there is plenty of food in there and you have got to be hungry so come on let me show you the place"

"Yes, I need to freshen up," said Ester as she reached into the back seat for her bag.

Frank lead them down a path to the front door at the right of the garage, it was a two story house with two gabled windows on the second floor. Frank opened the door and stood back and let Ester enter, the entrance opened onto a living room with a staircase on the right leading up to the second floor, on the left was an entrance to the kitchen that led to an enclosed patio. The patio opened to a fine view of a water front lake.

Ester followed Frank onto the patio and stood there with her arms folded gazing at the view, "it's beautiful, I can see why you wanted it." she comments.

"It was irresistible at the time.., it still is," Frank paused and then added, "I'm hungry but I also need a shower, come let me show you the master bedroom," he led her off the patio to the master bedroom on the ground floor talking as they walked, "I changed the linen on the bed when I left and there are fresh towels in the linen closet here," he indicated a closet door, "you must feel the need for a nap after sleeping in the car.., I will use the shower upstairs, just make yourself at home," he stood and let her enter the master bedroom, it had a beautiful view of the lake, "you should find everything you need," said Frank as he gathered up fresh underwear and a folded pair of Khaki trousers, he turned and started for the stairs to the upstairs bedroom, carrying his change of clothes.

Ester had the over night bag in her hand as she stood taking in the view of the lake.

Upstairs Frank had a quick shower, dressed in the Khaki trousers and a t-shirt, walked back downstairs rinsed the coffee maker, put in fresh coffee and turned it on.

Ester came out of the master bedroom and walked to the kitchen, she wore a fluffy white terry cloth bath robe, Frank watched her walk up to the counter separating the kitchen from the patio, her breast move under the robe, he knew she had no bra.

"My, my.., that robe has never looked so good, it looks like it was made especially for you." commented Frank.

Frank watched the movement of her breast as she climbed up on the stool, he could see the cleavage now.

"Thanks," said Ester, with a coy smile, "that coffee smells good."

"One cup coming right up," said Frank as he placed a mug in front of her and took the coffee pot off the machine and filled the mug, he moved the cream and sugar where she could reach it.., "M,m,m, that coffee is splendid," she said after a sip, "and I really needed it."

"Good, this bread just came out of the freezer but it should make good toast, and we have a frozen breakfast with eggs and sausage, you can have a choice of scrambled or scrambled, or if you prefer you can have oatmeal."

"Eggs will be fine," said Ester smiling.

Frank turned and put the eggs in the microwave and turned it on, he reached into the fridge and took out a jar of canned citrus fruit and began to spoon out two helpings.

"You do that like you have a lot experience, are you a chef?" Ask Ester.

"No, no," said Frank, "oh if it comes to starving or cooking, I can cook, but I really don't have the patience for it," he grinned at her.

"Well it's good to be able to do that," said Ester as she bent over and took another sip of the coffee.

Frank put the other frozen breakfast in the microwave and turned back just as Ester raised up from her coffee, he got another view of the cleavage, the robe was looser now.

Frank spooned the eggs and sausage on a plate, they looked less like a frozen dinner that way, he put the plate in front of Ester and turned for the other eggs then put bread in the toaster.

After spooning the second frozen breakfast on a plate, he put the plate next to Ester then turned and walked around the counter and sat next to her. They began to eat, the eggs and sausage on the plate rather then on the frozen food container improved the taste as well as looking more appetizing. it was a satisfying late breakfast or brunch. Frank took the last bite of eggs and buttered toast and reached for his coffee.

Ester finished her plate and said, "that was good and I didn't know how hungry I was."

"yes a little food always helps," Said Frank. They were just two people now with one house and one car, they finished the eggs and sat sipping the coffee.

Suddenly Ester said, "well I wonder if there will be another meteor or if that was the last one for a while?"

After pausing for a moment Frank speaks, "I have been studying the cosmos and this solar system in particular.., we have learned a very great deal about the solar system since we started sending robots out from Earth and with the new telescopes like Hubble in space," he comments.

"You don't hear a great deal about it in the news," she said.

"Yes that's true, the government and NASA for some reason don't put out a lot of information, they send out a robot to say Mars and they report back that the mission was successful, the robot is on Mars and is working but then if you want more information you have to dig it out. I think the media also has something to do with it, they may be afraid of boring their audience and then they also may be afraid of frightening the tax payer."

"Frightening the taxpayer?" she ask.

"Yes.., I think if the average citizen on planet earth knew how fragile and delicate his position here on planet Earth is it would scare some of the hell right out of him as they say."

"I don't understand," she said.

O. K. let's take Mars, Mars is about one half the size and mass of planet Earth, we have robots on the surface of Mars reporting back and we have robots in orbit around the planet.., India has a robot in orbit, looking exclusively for methane, methane is an almost sure sign of life, they have found some but they are pretty sure it is from the geology of the planet and they have been thinking planet Mars is a dying planet, well I believe it is already dead, I believe if there is any life on planet Mars it is underground or deep in caves.., Mars has one of the highest mountains in the solar system and it is made up of molten lava and there are other molten domes all over the planet," he paused for a moment and then continued.

"Millions of years ago Mars had an atmosphere very similar to Earth's," he continued, "it had water and clouds and oxygen and erupting volcanos, the erupting volcano's sent all the heat into frozen space and slowly the molten core became solid and it no longer produced a magnetic shield that protected the planet's atmosphere and the solar wind and radiation from the sun dried up the water and blew away the atmosphere leaving a dried up dusty desert of a planet." he paused.., "of course it was not that simple, it is more complicated then that and there are things going on there now that have not been explained."

He had her full attention now, she was making eye contact and she took a sip of coffee when he paused.

"Let's get back to planet Earth," he said after a sip of his coffee.

"One of the great tragedies of planet Earth was the catastrophe that occurred at Pompeii, an ancient city on the Gulf Of Naples, Mt.Vesuvius, a volcanic mountain erupted in AD 79, killing thousands, maybe hundreds of thousands of people, they have no way of knowing how many, the lava flow just covered the whole city.., now in spite of that tragedy and other similar eruptions around the planet, the lava eruptions and flows are the planet's life blood, because without the Earths molten core the planet would have no magnet shield and our future would look like the planet Mars.

"Oh my," she said beginning to stir in her seat.

"Oh.., I'm sorry, I didn't mean to frighten you." He Said.

"No, it's O.K., we go through life assuming things and never really questioning where these words of authority came from or what they are based on."

"Yes, I know exactly what you are saying," he answered, "I was reading, the ancient Greeks studied the stars and planets and concluded in all revolved around planet Earth, (geocentrism) but as early as the 3rd. century B.C. a Greek by the name of Aristarchus proposed that the earth revolved around the Sun (heliocentric) but this was ignored, possibly because of a loss of scientific works in the Hellenistic era and it wasn't until Copernicus was born in 1473 AD that Copernicus published, let's say, and Galileo with his telescope proved the theory of Heliocentric, that it was accepted."

"ALL that time and possible discoveries were lost because everybody was going down the wrong path," she said.

"The amazing thing is how many discoveries and new things are found while we are looking at something else, you are right," he said, "luckily some have been able to make new discoveries while under the influence of a wrong theory."

There was a pause and then he continued, "do you know about tectonic plates?"

"Vaguely, we are sitting on these plates that are constantly moving."

"Yes the Earth's crust is only about ten miles thick and below that is the molten core.," he began to explain, "but let's get back to the beginning.., about four billions years ago there was a big bang and Earth was a comet or a large astroid flying thru space and it collided with another flying body and they coalesced and continued to spin and all the heavy metals were pushed to the center and the pressure created a molten core, the planet continued to spin and hit and be hit and it continued to grow and the Sun captured it and the molten core created a magnetic field that shielded the atmosphere from the solar wind and the solar radiation and the Earth's gravity held the atmosphere."

"Wow, that is a logical and believable answer," she comments.

"It is, but so far they have not been able to prove it, like taking water and freezing it solid or putting fire under it and watch it boil, turn to steam and disappear in the atmosphere," he explained.

"No but it is a very logical explanation," she said.

"Well yes and they have parts of it proven and they are heading in that direction, so to speak, they can not prove the big bang theory but they have evidence pointing to that's what happened," he explained, "but let's get back to Earth, we are on the crust or tectonic plates and when the plates meet, they do not collide, one plate moves under the other and when that happens we feel earthquakes and tsunamis."

"Wow, yes, I can see the logic of that, I never thought about it before, but I can understand it," she said.

"That's true, now take Iceland, that island has three tectonic plates that come together under it and there are four major, large, volcanos there and many smaller ones under the ice, it was just one that erupted recently and it disrupted the airlines and the European economy, jet engines can not fly through volcanic ash, but that one eruption threw ash into the atmosphere and blocked the sun for weeks over Europe," he said and after a pause he continued, "now in the Pacific northwest of this country there are four major volcanos and many smaller ones, Yellowstone National Park is sitting on a caldera that is more then fifty miles wide, a caldera is the mouth of the volcano where the vent opens into the atmosphere and Old Faithful is there to remind us whats under our feet," he paused for a moment and took a sip of his coffee.

She took a sip giving him her full attention.

He continued, "now if the big four volcanos on the west coast and Yellowstone erupted together, throwing ash clouds into the atmosphere and the jet stream joined in spreading ash clouds over the northern hemisphere, it could last for months and even years and you have another ice age, now the skeptics will say, 'ah that will never happen again, those volcanos are all dormant,' they would have bet serious money that Mt. St, Helen on the west coast was dormant and it would not erupt again and that was true until it did, now if the tectonic plates under Iceland moved and the four big volcanos erupted and the four volcanos on our west coast erupted and the jet stream joined in covering the northern hemisphere with ash clouds, agriculture would come to a halt in Canada, the US and Europe and then what would this over populated earth eat?"

"We never think about those things, we assume whoever is in charge is looking after things," she comments.

"Volcanos are not the only reason to be concerned, Solar Flares from the Sun could knock out the power grid," he paused looking at her, she was still giving him her full attention.

"The Sun gives off Solar Flares all the time some bigger then others, but they are not all pointed at earth, some are pointed away from Earth and they just flare off into space, occasionally a flare will be pointed directly at Earth when it goes off and it can cause a lot of havoc on the technology here on Earth, the last big flare that was pointed at earth was about the mid 1800's there were not a lot of radio's, telephones or a power grid so it did not do a lot of damage, of course if you were laying out on a beach in a bikini when the flare arrived you may have had a problem." he paused and took a sip.

"Don't they have some way to protect Earth from that?" she ask.

"Yes they have satellites at the sun and I am sure they can tell when a flare is coming and give a few hours notice but then I am not sure what else they can do, turn off the power grid and try to get everybody indoors, but planet Earth would still take a really big hit, and that is not the worse that could happen, We have the planets, Mercury, Venus, Earth, and Mars, these are known as the inner planets and out past Mars we have Jupiter, Saturn, Uranus and Neptune, these are known as the outer planets. We had a ninth planet, Pluto but they decided it is not large enough to qualify as a planet so they are calling Pluto a dwarf planet and so we will concentrate on the four inner planets and the four outer planets.., between Mars and the gas giant Jupiter, we have the Kuiper belt. The kuiper belt is a belt or band of space debris, that ranges all the way from tiny dust particles to Asteroids a half mile and more across. The tiny dust particles are the shooting stars you see at night when they enter our atmosphere and burn up. Out past the Kuiper belt we have the Oort cloud. The Oort cloud is similar to the Kuiper belt only it is much larger and it reaches all the way out to the edge of the solar system and it has some of the largest debris out there ranging all the way up to planet Pluto size."

He paused for another sip and then continued..,

"There are thousands of asteroids that are more then one half mile across and we have always been grateful for the gas giant planet Jupiter for pulling any passing flyers into it, and it has done that but recently we have found it can also kick an astroid or meteor down into the inner planets, it would only take one of those rocks one half a mile or more across slamming into planet Earth to put a stop to most of the life on this planet."

"Oh my goodness," she said as she held her cup in both hands.

"Yes they have found an impact crater in southern Mexico and they are thinking this may have been the one that put an end to the Dinosaurs on this planet or it could have been that one plus others that landed in the ocean, at any rate it put an end to most of the life on this planet at that time."

Suddenly Frank slid off his stool, walked around the counter and began to collect the dishes and put them in the sink, Ester slid off her stool, "here let me do that," she said as she walked around the counter, with the close confine of the space between the sink, stove and counter and with the last of the dishes in the sink, Ester's breast brushed against his upper arm, he turned, they were very close, he looked into her eyes.., "look, I don't want to make you do anything you don't want to do, but if you are in the mood, I have some fresh prophylactics."

Ester very close now whispered, "I think I am in the mood."

THE END

Printed in the United States
By Bookmasters